OSPREY ON O'SHAUGHNESSY RESERVOIR

An Emma Haines
Kayak Mystery

By

TRUDY
BRANDENBURG

This book is a work of fiction. Names, characters, organizations, companies, and incidents are products of the author's imagination or, if real, are used fictitiously. Any resemblance to actual persons, living or dead, or to events, is entirely coincidental.

All rights reserved. No part of this book may be reproduced or transmitted in any form or by any means, electronic or mechanical, including photocopying, recording, or by any information storage and retrieval system, without the written permission of the author.

Photo Cover: O'Shaughnessy Reservoir
Photograph by Trudy Brandenburg

OSPREY ON O'SHAUGHNESSY RESERVOIR
Copyright © 2019 by Trudy Brandenburg
All rights reserved.

ISBN: 9781090193223

*Dedicated to our basset hound, Millie.
We miss you, baby girl.*

Saturday, July 19, 2014

"I LOVE KAYAKING. Why didn't you take me sooner? I've asked you for years," Clintonville police Lieutenant Joey Reed asked. He turned his kayak toward Emma Haines.

She squinted. "I didn't think you'd like it."

"Why not?"

She named the favorite of her five kayaks *Arlene* after a friend who passed away years earlier. Arlene purchased the kayak for her because she'd helped her during her illness. Emma laid her paddle across *Arlene's* cockpit and gave Joey a disgruntled look. "You're not an outdoor kind of guy. You're always working and chasing women."

"Not anymore. I'm settling down."

"And I'm running for president," she said. "Look, I honestly thought you'd end up whining and telling me how to kayak, and I've been paddling for twenty years."

"Are you insinuating that I'm a know-it-all?" He laid the paddle across the boat cockpit, stretched, and yawned. His black curls hung from under his ball cap and lifted in a breeze. He crossed his arms in front of his chest. His dark eyes glinted as he gave her a pouty look.

"I don't have to tell you something you already know," she said through a laugh. "But I'm glad you like kayaking."

"Yeah. It's pretty cool. But getting up at six on a Saturday morning off isn't my idea of fun," he said.

"I wanted to get out here early to beat the heat, the fishermen, and the boaters. It's quieter. Peaceful."

Joey looked around. "Yeah, I guess you're right. Supposed to get in the mid-nineties again today. Boats will be buzzing all over the place later. I see your point." He paused before he said, "Women will dig it when I tell them that I kayak. You can always loan me another boat, right?"

"Wait. I thought you were settling down."

"I am, when I find the right woman."

"Yeah, right. I'm not sure you're going to find her at the gentlemen's club," Emma said as she paddled out ahead of him, shaking her head.

He caught up with her. "When is Stratton coming back from Europe?"

Emma shrugged. "I don't know. His agent keeps finding more places for him to speak and have book signings. He wants to do as much as he can while he's there."

"That makes sense. So why didn't you stay over there with him?"

"I'm just not a Europe kind of girl, I guess. I mean, it's a nice place to visit, but it's not home. I was alone a lot there. Stratton was busy, and I got tired of being a lone tourist. It's okay. He'll be home soon," she said.

"I've traveled abroad, and I get that. It's not home," he said.

They paddled lazily around the inlet known as Twin Lakes, then through the large metal culvert under Route

745. A few small docks jutted into the water from the houses that sat on the rise to their left. They passed a kayak club to their right. They came to the opening of O'Shaughnessy Reservoir and stopped.

O'Shaughnessy Reservoir is a north-south waterway formed by a dam on the Scioto River near Glick Road in Delaware County, Ohio. It covers nearly nine hundred acres and has around eighteen miles of shoreline. It was built in 1925 and remains a water source for Columbus. Its deepest points are around forty feet.

Emma turned and watched Joey paddle toward her. "You look good in that boat. You're getting the hang of it. Hey! Look over there to your right, up in the sky," Emma said, nodding that way and paddling beside him. She grabbed the side of his kayak.

"Wah! That thing went all the way into the water and shot back out. Look! It's got a fish in its toenails," Joey said, putting his right hand on his ball cap rim to shield his eyes from the sun.

"Those aren't toenails. They're talons. That's an osprey. They're also known as river hawks, and often they go all the way under the water to catch a fish and then …" The bird threw the fish in the air and caught it, carrying it like a torpedo. "Did you see that?" Emma asked.

"Yeah," Joey said. "Cool."

"They fly with the fish like a torpedo—less drag. They're the only bird that can flip its back talon around to hold its food, sort of like our thumb. It'll sit in a tree and eat," Emma said.

"I had no idea. I never pay attention to birds," he said.

"Most people never pay attention to the nature that's around them every day, especially if they're in the city.

Most people don't even see birds. They'd feel better if they did. Birds are dinosaurs, you know? Running around with us all the time. There'd be so many more bugs if there weren't any birds, and birds are food for other animals. All part of that food chain. Nature is healing. It can also be nasty. Anyway, you've seen your first osprey catch. Congratulations. They're gorgeous. Next spring I'll take you to Alum and we'll watch the parents feed their babies on the nesting platforms through binoculars."

"That'd be neat," he said.

They watched the bird fly out of sight with its breakfast. A flock of Canada geese flew over them in their typical "V" formation. They both looked up.

"What are those big flappy things?" Joey asked.

"Seriously? You don't know?"

Joey shook his head. "No."

"Those 'big flappy things' are Canada geese."

"I think I've seen some before. Yeah, I have seen them before. And I knew they were geese," he said in a low voice.

"Probably. There's a few around." She smiled to herself.

Joey turned his boat. "I want to paddle to the zoo."

"That's not a good idea. We've been out here for an hour, and we have to paddle back. You're using muscles you didn't know you had, even if you do work out. Let's go back. Too big of water for you right now. I'll buy us breakfast at the Wildflower."

"I'll be fine." He turned his kayak and started paddling into the reservoir.

Emma protested, but he ignored her. She finally gave up and sat in her boat as she watched him pull farther ahead. He grew smaller in the distance, gliding across the water. He was a strong paddler, and she knew he could swim. *He'll be fine,* she thought.

She glanced at the blue sky and the bright sun, out to fulfill the ninety-five-degree forecast.

A great blue heron flew overhead. She loved them. They always reminded her of pterodactyls. Along the shoreline, tree swallows performed crazy acrobatics, catching their breakfast of bugs. Far off, a kingfisher chattered. She wondered if Joey would notice birds more now. At the moment, he was on a mission to get to the shores of the Columbus Zoo and Aquarium.

To her right, toward the dam, the sound of an engine starting caught her attention. She watched a speedboat putter out into the open water. The sun glinted off its windshield for a split second. She couldn't make out who was under the boat's dark canopy. It was the only boat she saw that morning.

An early fisherman, she thought. Suddenly, the boat's bow leaped into the air. In seconds, the boat barreled across the water. *But we're in a no-wake zone. Maybe the boat driver wasn't familiar with the area,* she thought.

"Joey! A boat! Watch out for the boat! It's going to make waves. Joey! Joey!" She grabbed the emergency whistle that hung from her life jacket and blew it hard, trying to get Joey's and the boat driver's attention, but she was too far away. She waved her yellow paddle in the air. She started paddling as fast as she could toward Joey, hoping the speedboat would stop or at least see him and veer around him. But the boat turned and barreled toward him.

Joey! Joey!" she yelled. "JOOOOOOEEEEY!" she screamed as the speedboat plowed over Joey Reed and sped away.

***

Merek sat on his leather couch. He sipped CrimsonCup coffee he'd brewed for breakfast and eyed his Samsung cellphone on the glass coffee table in front of him. He ran a hand over his buzz-cut brown hair and sighed. He stood, walked to the glass wall of his living room, and looked down. The Olentangy River was low, barely a trickle, sparkling like a gray sequin snake.

He wondered how Joey's first kayak trip was going with Emma on O'Shaughnessy Reservoir. He imagined a bit of arguing, as Merek considered them both "control freaks," but they always seemed to come to terms in the end. He sipped coffee as he gazed out the window, his thoughts shifting from Emma to his recent stay in Warsaw, Poland. He had returned four months ago after a two-year visit.

His parents were aging, and he had planned on staying. He was the oldest son of three. Emma told him to stay, too. She joked that she could tell people she worked at H.I.T.'s international headquarters in Clintonville, Ohio, where they lived, with a branch office in Poland, run by the firm's partner, Merek Polanski. But he didn't work while he was there. He helped his parents around the house and argued continually with his younger brothers. The visit had been a catastrophe.

His parents and brothers insisted he return to his "happy American life." They said that's where he belonged—not in Poland. And his two younger brothers were there to look after them. It seemed like everyone wanted him to leave, and he did miss his American life. He missed his high-rise condo that he'd sublet while he was in Poland. He missed his Harley. He missed his friends. He missed his job. He missed many things about America. So he returned. But lately, he had not been happy in America, even though he enjoyed being Emma's partner at H.I.T.

H.I.T. stood for Haines Insurance Training. Emma had started the firm seventeen years ago. Merek had met her at a computer supply store. She asked him to be her office manager, and they walked out of the store together. He never looked back. Later, Emma made him an official company partner. She and Merek worked together to train insurance investigators. Their main client was Matrix Insurance.

She had worked at Matrix for over twenty years, advancing through the ranks to become an insurance fraud investigator. She enjoyed her work until an affluent policyholder—and so-called financial baron—named Dayton Kotmister burned down his family estate and took a shot at her while she was questioning him at the scene.

She had helped put Kotmister away for a second time two years ago. After plotting his revenge, Kotmister struck as Emma and her sexagenarian beau, Stratton Reeves, were kayaking on the Red River. Kotmister took Stratton at gunpoint and ran over Emma with a monster truck. Amazingly, she survived with no more than scratches and a sore butt, and Stratton was rescued unharmed. They later learned that Kotmister had also ordered the killing of her dear friend Charles's former partner, Simon.

Stratton wrote a book about the incident and it became a best-seller. He was an award-winning journalist and owned *The Stonefalls Post*, a small newspaper in West Virginia. Emma met him three years ago while she was pursuing a criminal that she and Charles had, unfortunately, ran into on the New River while kayaking.

But Merek was lonely and weary of dating. And he couldn't get a woman he called "New York Natalie" off his mind. He didn't understand why she had made such an impression on him. They met once briefly while he was helping Emma and Charles look for Stratton. She had been singing a beautiful song while she was cleaning a run-down, closed gas station near Derby Crossing, Kentucky. Her parents had owned it before they died. She grew up there, but moved to New York City to attend college, but she never finished because she married and started a family. Merek told her she should go back to college to get her music degree. Days after he returned, she called him and told him that she'd taken his advice.

He often dreamed about Natalie; her shoulder-length, ebony hair swaying as she turned her head, her bright red lipstick smile, the long, red fingernail as she ran it along the edge of his business card. And he could still hear her singing—that beautiful voice.

She reeked of New York City, money, and class—not his type of woman. He wondered where she was now and if she had finished her music degree. But mostly he wondered if she was still married to her husband, who told her that she sang too much. He thought of her nearly every day and could never bring himself to delete her number from his phone.

Since his return from Poland, he had dated a few women. They all fit the same basic description—blonde and beautiful. Two worked as pole dancers at *The Messenger Club*. Another owned a chain of spas, and another lived off a rich ex-husband's alimony. And they all bored him. Every time he was with one of them, he thought about Natalie. And all he did was shake her hand and talk with her for a few minutes. *Funny how some people just stick with you—no matter what,* he thought. He walked across the room and picked up the Samsung.

He examined his reflection in the small, black screen. The rows of silver earrings in both ears and eyebrow rings reflected in the light. The colorful tattoos on his neck looked like black and white sketches in the phone's screen, the bright colors of the ink not showing.

He touched the screen several times and the phone number of "New York Natalie" appeared. His finger hovered over the phone.

"It is time," he said in Polish. He took a deep breath, closed his eyes, and touched the screen.

***

Merek had fallen asleep on the couch. On his seventy-two-inch television screen, the Saturday afternoon ESPN sports show announcers sat around a mahogany desk, making millions of dollars arguing over a moot point of a baseball play. Merek was jolted awake by his ringing phone. He sat up, muted the television, grabbed the phone, and looked at its screen. "Miss H."

"Merek, can you please come to Riverside Hospital? Joey was run over by a speedboat while we were kayaking. I'm here, but they took him into surgery. Can you come?" Emma said in a shaky voice.

"*Tak*, Miss H. I will be there." He ended the call and changed into a pair of black leather pants and a T-shirt. He grabbed his Harley keys and biker jacket and ran out of his condo toward the elevator. He punched the button and paced. The chains rattled on his boots as he walked.

Thirty minutes later, he sat beside Emma in the hospital's waiting area. "He will be okay, Miss H?" Merek asked.

She shrugged and wiped her nose with a tissue. "I hope so. A couple of fishermen helped us. They called 911, and the squad was waiting for us."

Merek rubbed her back. "I am so sorry, Miss H. Tell me what happened."

"This speedboat came out of nowhere and ran over him, then sped up and took off. It looked deliberate to me."

"A hit and run?" he asked.

"I guess that's what you'd call it," she said.

"What did this boat look like? Tell me everything."

"Okay. Could you please write down what I tell you? I already talked to the police, but this will help, too." She dug a pen and notebook out of her cross-body Fossil purse and handed it to him. "Maybe I'll think of something else while we're talking."

Merek asked questions and jotted down her replies. They sat and waited. Two hours later, a nurse approached them.

"Mr. Reed is in recovery. He can't have visitors, and I can't tell you much since you're not family."

"Will he be okay?" Emma asked.

The nurse took Emma's hands in hers and smiled sadly. "I can't give you any details, sweetie. But he is awake and talking—a lot. He said he does want to see you, but not tonight. I'm sorry. That's about all I can say."

Emma laughed through her tears. "Yeah, he's a talker. That's good news." She smiled and nodded. "I understand. When *can* I see him?"

"Call first. I just don't know."

Sunday

SUNDAY MORNING, SEVERAL members of the Southern Ohio Floaters Association, also called SOFA, founded in Chillicothe, Ohio, stood in the Wildflower Café parking lot. They had met there for breakfast and their vehicles carried a kayak on the roof or in a truck bed. Emma was originally from Chillicothe and she and her friend Charles occasionally kayaked with SOFA.

She'd put the word about Joey's accident on the club's Facebook page before she went to bed. She needed more eyes to help her look for that boat. She'd call the hospital again later to see when she could visit Joey. She had to do something in the meantime.

"So, again, we're looking for a white boat with a windshield and a dark canopy. If you see one docked at a house, note the location. The canopy could be rolled up or something, so just note the location of any white boats with a windshield," Emma said to the group.

"The canopy's called a Bimini. Or they could've gotten rid of it, hid it, sold it, or sunk it," someone yelled.

"True. But it doesn't hurt to try," Emma said.

"Right, and it's a beautiful day to be on the water

together," someone else yelled.

"And remember, if anyone asks, we're all in a bird-watching club," Emma reminded them, holding up a pair of binoculars. "Okay, let's go."

All the kayakers, except for Emma and Sharon, headed to O'Shaughnessy Reservoir to launch at different boat ramps around the lake. The two women stood at the same boat launch where Emma and Joey had put their kayaks on the lake yesterday morning.

"Sort of a long shot for sure doing this, don't you think?" Sharon asked.

Emma shrugged. "Doesn't hurt. And remember what you always say, 'Any day on the water is a good day.' And if we just happen to find that boat, it will be a *really* good day."

"That's right," Sharon replied. "How's your friend doing?"

"He's talking, and that's good. But that's all I know. I feel like it was my fault," Emma said. "I should've never let him go out there."

Sharon leaned over and hugged her. "It's not your fault. It just happened. It was an accident."

"I should've never let him go out on the big water."

Sharon hugged her harder. "It's not your fault," she repeated.

Three hours later, the group stood around the Twin Lakes parking lot. "So what do we have?" Emma asked. "Anyone see a white boat with a windshield and a canopy or, sorry, a Bimini?"

Two people raised a hand.

"Okay. Let's have it," Emma said, nodding her head toward Jane.

"I saw two," Jane said. "I sketched their locations on

the lake from here and wrote down the tag numbers of the boats." She ripped a piece of paper from a notepad and handed it to Emma. "White boats with windshields."

"Bimini?" Emma asked.

"It looked like one had a blue one rolled up."

"And the other?" Emma asked.

"No canopy thing, but it was a white boat with a windshield."

"Thanks, Jane."

Rose spoke up. "I talked to a man mowing his lawn. He said that boaters know to look out for other boats, including kayaks. He read about the accident in the paper. He thought it was odd that it happened. He suggested someone boating under the influence of alcohol or drugs. Or had a heart attack and lost control at the wheel."

Emma jotted in her notebook. "Those are great points. We have to consider all possibilities until we have the facts. I can get the heart attack angle checked out through the hospitals."

Loren said, "I saw two white boats with windshields but no Biminis. Here's the tag numbers."

"Thanks. Anyone else?"

No one replied. "Okay. I can't thank you all enough for coming here and helping," Emma said.

"I hope your friend recovers fast and you find out who did it," someone said. Everyone wished Emma and Joey well as they headed to their vehicles to go home.

"Me, too," Emma said. "Me, too."

***

"I'm sorry, Joey. I should've never let you go out into that open water. This is terrible," Emma said as she looked at the casts on his left arm and leg. His face was bruised and he had a big bump on his forehead and several cracked ribs. He told her the lights were low in the room because he had a concussion, and that he would be in the hospital for several days for tests and observation.

"They just want to make sure my head didn't get too rattled. Anyway, like you could've stopped me. *I'm sorry*. I'll buy you another boat, okay? Let's just get to the meat of this thing and not wallow in it. It happened. It was no one's *fault*. Let's find out who did it and move on." He grimaced as he propped himself higher on his pillow. "Did you see what the boat looked like? The build, make, tag, driver, anything?"

"You sure you want to talk about this now? You're probably pretty drugged up and in pain, aren't you?" she said.

He shook his head. "I refused the heavy-duty meds. So, yeah, I hurt, and I've got a hell of a headache. I see spots now and then, too. But we need to talk about it while it's still fresh. You know that."

She paused. "I know. Okay. I remember a few things. Here's what I told the officers yesterday afternoon when they questioned me." She pulled her notebook from her purse and flipped it open. "It all happened so fast. The boat came out of a little inlet near the dam. It was white and had a windshield and a Bimini. That's what the canopy over the driver is call. But I couldn't make out the driver at all. It came out really slow, then went flying upstream in a no-wake zone. I have no idea what it was doing in there going that fast. It wasn't a big boat. And I didn't see any engine sticking up on the back, so likely an inboard motor. That's what one of the officers said who I talked with. It's not much, but ... Joey, you just ..." Her shoulders dropped, and she tilted her head toward him. "You could've been killed."

"You do remember that I'm a cop, right?"

"Yeah, I know. But ... anyway, that boat had plenty of time to see you and there was room for him to go around you. But it swerved toward you, then sped up after it hit you."

The room went quiet.

"Who questioned you?"

She looked back at her notes. "Miles and Rigs."

"Good guys." He sighed. "You think someone ran over me on purpose?"

"That's how it looked. You've busted a lot of bad guys over the years. Maybe someone's got it out for you who owns a speedboat. But how would they know it was you out there? If they didn't see you, they had to see me. And even if they never saw us, they'd likely have swerved to miss you and they had to feel *something* when they ran over you—like hitting a log or something. They should've stopped. I'd hate to think it was just some idiot getting their early-morning jollies by running over a kayaker," she said.

"Doesn't make sense. How *would* they know it was me or that I'm a cop? If they wanted to kill me, why wouldn't they just shoot me instead of taking a risk of someone seeing them? That's a big risk to take if you're trying to knock someone off. You tell anyone we were kayaking?" he asked.

Emma shook her head. "No. And I don't post anything on Facebook anymore, except I asked SOFA for their help on their Facebook page last night.

"Maybe it was just hit and run fear after they realized what they did. Partiers. Drunk. Drugs. Who knows?

Merek checked the local hospitals but didn't find any reports that might be connected to the accident. The kayak club paddled around the area this morning, too, looking for the boat. Here's what we found." She tore sheets from her notebook and handed them to him.

"That was nice of Merek and the club. Thank them for me. Always good to go back to the scene. You're a good investigator, Emma. I'll have the boat numbers checked."

"I learned from the best. What do you remember?" she asked.

"Not much. By the time I realized what was happening I was under the water. I remember looking up and seeing the front of this boat and the next thing—*Wham!* Nothing but water and waves after that. It hit me from the side. I don't remember. It happened so fast. I should've listened to you and not gone over there."

They sat in silence before Joey said, "It's a good thing those fishermen stopped and helped us. I was lucky. I know that. And stupid. I know that, too."

"Glad you had on your life jacket. Even though you're busted up pretty bad, it could've been a lot worse. My kayak only has a few scuff marks on it from the accident. That's it. I don't know if the boat would have any damage or marks, but from what Miles said, it probably wouldn't."

She looked at his arm and leg casts. "How long do you have to stay in the hospital?" she asked.

He shrugged. "They're not really saying. They don't want me to put any weight on my leg for a few days." He threw his head back on his pillow and let out a long breath. "This may be a looooong summer. I'm starting to itch already," he muttered, scratching himself under his arm cast.

"Maybe you'll meet some good-looking nurses who'll scratch you."

He turned to her. "Now you're talking." He grinned that Joey Reed grin that melted many a woman's heart. But never Emma's. Joey certainly was an attractive guy—thick, black curly hair, graying now at the sides—big brown eyes. But there was never a spark between them other than good investigative work. Together, they'd solved many insurance fraud cases and Joey had helped Emma put away a few bad guys on the side, too.

Joey went through women as fast as Merek. A few of them were even the same women—dancers at the *Messenger Club*, which the two men frequented.

Emma looked at the clock and yawned. She slid her notebook in her purse and closed it. "I'm sorry, again," she said. "You need to rest, and it's almost ten. I need to get home and take Millie for a walk."

Joey closed his eyes. "She's probably snoring on her couch."

"That's what bassets do. Okay, I'm outta here. I'll be back tomorrow." She stood.

He asked, "You still have Maggie?"

Maggie was Stratton's golden retriever. "No. She's with Rhonda and her husband down in West Virginia, at Stratton's. They wanted to keep her while Stratton's on his book tour, so Millie and I drove her down several weeks ago. It's a better place for her to run."

He nodded and yawned.

She placed a hand on his shoulder. "Hopefully, someone saw something that can help us find the driver of that boat. Maybe someone along the bank fishing or walking will call the station with information."

"I hope so. I'd like to talk to the guy that ruined my first kayak trip."

"Or gal. You ditched any babes lately?" she asked, jokingly.

He blinked and frowned. "As a matter of fact ..." He trailed off before explaining.

"Fantasy? The same Fantasy that Merek dumped before he left for Poland?" Emma asked.

"Yeah. So? They dated a couple years ago, Emma."

"I just don't get it with you guys. I don't get in your business. But don't you think you're getting too old for this?"

"For what?" he asked.

"Oh, come on, Joey. You and Merek aren't twenty years old anymore. You're nearly fifty and he's almost thirty. I thought you said you were done with pole dancers and crazy chicks and you were settling down. From what I hear, she's both—and not someone you'd want to mother your children. And sharing them? That's sort of ... weird." She made a face.

"Who said anything about children? And we don't *share* them. You make us sound like ... I don't know what. Yeah, so, we've dated a few of the same women. So what? And Fantasy has a classy job. She's waiting tables at Brown's. That's a five-star restaurant. That's where I saw her again. She quit the club awhile back."

Emma frowned at him.

"You wouldn't understand. You're a one-man woman. I always admired you for that. But it never worked for me."

"Yippee for me. Look where it got me. A busted heart that finally healed, for a man who spends most of his time on book tours because he was kidnapped while he was on a kayaking trip with me. Whoopee."

"Oh, calm down. You've got it made. You could be with him. You're the one that came home. He'll be back soon, right?"

Emma stood. Her petite one-hundred and twenty-five-pound frame glided across the hospital room. Her Skechers squeaked on the polished floor. She gazed out the window into the parking garage, her back to Joey. She shoved her hands into the back pockets of her khakis.

"What? Don't tell me you two are having problems," he said.

"Everyone has problems. It's the way of the world."

"Talk to me, Emma."

"Nothing to say." She paused. She turned and faced him. "You consider your girl, Fantasy, a suspect?"

"First off, she's not *my girl*. I told you, I had to threaten her with a restraining order to leave me alone. She was pissed. But she's nuts. She called or texted me constantly. And I mean CONSTANTLY. She even showed up at the station a couple times—unannounced. My private life is my private life. I don't mix the two. I tried to explain that to her, and she got mad. She said I was ashamed of her."

Silence.

"Were you?" she asked.

"Were I what?"

"Ashamed of her?"

"I date lots of women. You know that. I don't want any of them bugging me or coming to the station. That's all."

"She have a speedboat?"

"Don't think so. But I wouldn't be surprised if she knows *someone* who does."

"But how would she know you were out there kayaking with me? You didn't tell anyone, did you?" Emma asked.

"No. Well ..." Joey trailed off and sighed.

"Well, what?"

"It was an accident. I thought I was texting you to confirm our plans, but I accidentally texted her instead. I'd had a few beers at home." He inhaled and frowned. "When I realized what I'd done, I sent her a text and apologized, told her it was a mistake, and then I texted you."

"Ahhhhh, Joey. I can't believe ..." Emma said as she ran her fingers through her shoulder-length, brunette hair and paced the floor.

"Yeah, I know. You don't have to tell me. Stupid. I should've deleted her out of my phone, but I didn't. I meant to, believe me. It just slipped my mind."

"You still have the text?"

"No. I deleted it. But they can pull that stuff if it comes to that. God, I hope not. Some of our texts were pretty ..."

Emma raised both hands. "Don't tell me. I don't want to know. You going to tell the cops about this?"

He didn't answer.

"Oh, come on, Joey."

"How many things have I done for you that could've cost me my job? If you find out something relevant, then I'll tell them. If not, no need to mention it. That's all."

"Did you ask Merek if *he* was with her Saturday?" she said, sarcastically.

"That's cold. Give me a break. No pun intended," he said, glancing at himself. He turned toward the window. He wished it wasn't a few feet away from the parking garage, but at least he had a window. Several cars lumbered down the ramp, their passengers likely leaving from visiting loved ones in the hospital.

"Did you tell anyone else we were going kayaking?" she asked.

Joey and Emma had done this for years—questioning each other—figuring out the "who, what, when, and where" together on dozens of cases.

"I told a couple of the guys at work the other day. That's all."

"What other day?"

He closed his eyes. "Thursday. Yeah. It was last Thursday. Right before lunch. We were sitting around my office, and they were having a good laugh about it. They felt like you. They couldn't imagine me kayaking."

Emma asked, "Who were *they*?"

"Cook and Sammy."

"They own any boats?" Emma asked.

Joey shook his head. "No. And they're not suspects, so don't even go there."

"Okay. Anyone else hear you?"

He shook his head.

"Fantasy have a real name?" Emma asked.

"Fae Vernon. I'll tell you everything I know about her."

She sat down on the orange plastic chair again, pulled the notebook from her purse and started writing.

Twenty minutes later Joey said, "That covers it. You and Merek work with Miles when you need information. I'll call him."

"Okay," Emma said, flipping the notebook shut and putting it back in her bag. She yawned and stood. "I'll talk to you later. Get some rest."

She left and walked down the hallway. "Cameras," she whispered to herself as she glanced toward one, hanging in the corner from the ceiling.

Monday

THE MONDAY MORNING sunshine streamed through the slits in the drawn blinds into Joey's dark room as Merek tapped on the door. "Merek. Come on in, my man."

The chains on Merek's motorcycle boots clinked as he sauntered into the room. "You made the front page of the Sunday paper, Mr. Joey," his Polish accent thicker after his two-year stay. Merek handed Joey the paper. Joey turned on the hospital light above his bed and started to read.

Merek pulled a chair from against the wall, turned it backward facing the bed, and sat down, straddling it. He set a cup of CrimsonCup coffee on the side table and unzipped his black leather jacket. He picked up the cup and took a drink.

Still reading, Joey said, "That coffee smells good."

"Smaczny. It is the best. From the Clintonville shop.*"*

"I hate that picture of me," Joey said.

Merek looked him over. "You have more important worries than a picture. You look like *gówno.*"

"I don't know much Polish, but Emma told me what

that means. She says it a lot. Thanks, I know I look like shit."

Merek snickered.

The two men sat in silence while Joey reread the article. Finally, he turned to Merek.

"Emma call you right after the accident?"

"*Tak*. You were in surgery."

"I can imagine what she had to say."

Merek raised an eyebrow. Light glinted off the silver ring. He sipped his coffee.

"Yeah, I figured she'd sound off to you and Charles and probably Stratton. I can't blame her, though. I didn't listen to her."

Merek looked around the room.

"Did you have a good breakfast?" Merek asked.

"It was okay. At least I'm on not a restricted diet. Hint. Hint. Maybe you can get the word out. I love Big Macs."

"I will tell Emma," Merek said.

More silence.

"Emma tell you about Fantasy?"

Meek nodded, but didn't say anything.

"You haven't seen her lately, have you? I mean, it's cool if you have. Just asking."

"No. I have not seen or heard from her since I left for Poland. I heard about you two. And that she quit the club. Emma said that you want to check Fantasy out about this."

Joey looked back out the window for several seconds. "I only dated her for a few months, Merek. Chick is *way* too possessive. A few months back, I finally threatened her with a restraining order. She like that with you?"

"*Tak*. That is one reason I broke it off with her. And

other women. She is beautiful and … But she is like a sticky burger."

They laughed.

"She is beautiful and lots of fun, for sure." Joey said.

Merek drank more coffee as silence seeped into the room. Finally, Joey said, "She ever come after you? Threaten you or anything after you broke up?"

Merek shook his head. "No. But the week I broke up with her, I left for Poland. She called me many times, but I did not answer. Then she stopped. I do not know if she knows I am back."

"Oh, she knows, all right." Joey chuckled. "She told me you were the worst man she'd ever met."

"I am probably on a long list. With you," Merek said.

"Yeah, probably. I'd like to know where she was Saturday."

Merek finished his coffee and tossed the cup in the trash, then fished it out. Joey gave him a questioning look.

"Must recycle."

"Got it. So, can I ask you something else?"

Merek shrugged.

"Why'd you come back from Poland? I mean, I'm glad you did. Emma was a little crazy there for a while with you and Charles leaving at the same time. She actually had to *work*. Then Stratton went off on his book tours. But … I just wondered, you know? Just curious."

Merek tapped the empty coffee cup with his fingers, stood, and walked to the window. He looked at the cars in the hospital parking garage. Again, he wondered why people bought vanity plates.

"I love America. And my job with Emma. My parents wanted me to leave. They say I belong here now. They are proud of me, being a business partner." He paused for several seconds. "But my brothers, they do not understand. We have grown far apart," he said more to himself than to Joey.

"Yeah, that happens. People grow apart, even when they're close," Joey said.

Merek turned abruptly. "I gotta scram."

"That's cool. Hey, thanks for stopping by."

Merek headed for the open doorway.

"Hey," Joey said.

Merek turned.

"You really don't think Fantasy is crazy enough to run over me with a boat, do you?"

"Wszystko jest mozliwe. Anything is possible."

***

Later that morning, Merek glanced out the H.I.T. office window at the welcomed rain. It had been hot and dry for several days. He sat at his desk working on another presentation for Matrix Insurance. Emma was going to talk about the new claims-training suggestions with Calvin Nelson next week.

Calvin was a big reason why H.I.T. made a lot of money from Matrix. He was not only in charge of claims there, but also crazy in love with Emma. Everyone knew it. No one discussed it, except when Calvin would hound her for dates and she would complain about it.

Merek's thoughts circled back to Joey Reed. He was glad he'd gone to visit him this morning. They weren't close, but they worked on cases together. He and Joey kept their distance, frequenting the same club and sometimes the same women. It was an unspoken pact between them.

This morning was the first time they talked about a woman they both dated. Fantasy. Merek wondered if she actually would run over Joey with a boat. She did have serious possession issues. He didn't think she was that crazy or owned a boat. But he agreed with Joey and Emma—she could know someone who did.

His cell rang and vibrated, jolting him out of his thoughts. He glanced down at the screen. It read "New York Natalie." His heart skipped a beat as he hit the accept call icon.

"Hello."

"Merek Polanksi?"

"*Tak*. I mean yes."

"This is Natalie Sage returning your call."

"Natalie. Yes. Hello. I am fine. How are you? I was just wondering how you were doing."

"How'd you get my cell number?" she asked.

Merek didn't want to tell her he saved the number for two years when she called him, soon after they'd met, to tell him she was going back to college because of their discussion. He also didn't tell her that he'd run a check on her from snapping her rental car plate in Kentucky. He was a thorough researcher. "I just happened to see it when I was cleaning out my phone log. I do not clean it out often." He wondered if she would buy that and if she were tech-savvy.

"I understand. I should clean out my old contacts, but I just never seem to find the time, and they pile up." They made more small talk before she told him she'd finished her music and voice degree. She told him about her kids. Kenny was six. Sally was four.

"I'm a single mom now. Divorced last year. Cliché. Normal. Boring. Marriage had been on the rocks for years, but we just stayed together because of the children. But we're all much happier now. Mike, my ex, remarried. The kids like her. I like her. We all like her kids. They live about five miles from us. It all happened pretty quickly for everyone. Life goes on, you know?"

Merek felt his face grow warm. He didn't know if it was hearing her voice again or the talk of marriage, divorce, children, and families—life events he knew nothing about. He stammered, "This is good, then?"

She laughed. "Yeah, it is good. You know, I really believe if you hadn't walked into my parents' store that day and told me to go back to college ... Angels come in all forms, I guess. You were sort of an angel for me.

"What about you? I read about the kidnapping and Stratton Reeves. And now he has a bestselling book about it. I read it. You're famous. And his girlfriend, your business partner, she was run over by a truck by the kidnapper. And that's why you came in the store, looking for the truck. How is she?"

"Emma. She is fine."

"That's good. I'm glad she's okay."

"You are still in New York City?" Merek asked.

"Yes. And you're still in ... Indiana?"

"Ohio." He said, feeling a pang of disappointment that she didn't remember.

"That's right. Clintonville."

She *did* remember. He perked up.

"*Tak*. I mean yes."

"I'm taking a new job next year, teaching music in a grade school. I'm excited about it. The kids sing in a community choir with me, too. For fun, I sing and play guitar at a few restaurants and bars on the weekends. I stay busy."

"You have such a beautiful voice. I remember."

"Thank you. You're so kind. What else has been going on in your life, Merek Polanski?"

"You too inspired me the day we met." He told her about his trip to Poland and why he returned.

They talked for nearly an hour before Natalie said, "Merek, I enjoy talking with you, but I have to go."

"I also enjoy talking with you, New York Natalie," he said.

Silence.

"Do you think we could talk again—soon?" she asked.

He sat straighter. "*Tak*. I would like that very much. I will call you again soon. When is a good time?"

"Anytime. If I don't answer, just leave me a message. It's perfectly fine."

"Yes. I will call you soon. Goodbye for now."

"How do you say goodbye in Polish?" she asked.

"Do widzenia."

"*Do widzenia,* Merek Polanski. You know something?" she said.

"What?"

"I'm glad you didn't delete my number. You know something else?"

"What?" he said, his heart beating in his ears.

"I love to say your name. Sometimes I even sing it."

He closed his eyes and held onto the edge of his desk. "Keep singing it with your beautiful voice, New York Natalie."

"I will. Talk to you soon, Merek Polanski." She sang his name. The call ended.

He leaned back in the office chair and clasped his hands behind his head. A huge smile grew across his face.

***

Emma sat behind the wheel of her truck and checked the address Joey had given her for Fae Vernon, better known as Fantasy. She looked from her notebook at the sign above the glass doors of the tall building that read "Tibet Luxury Condominiums" and back down at the address. Fantasy was a waitress. Emma knew that several high-powered CEOs lived here, the upper crust of Columbus. She shook her head. "Girl must be making some hefty tips," she said aloud.

She scowled through the windshield at the rain but decided not to grab the umbrella she kept in her Tacoma pickup. She got out of the truck and jogged into the marble lobby, got on an elevator larger than her living room—complete with a small love seat against a mirrored wall—and hit the button for the seventh floor. Joey told her that if she got there before noon, she'd probably wake Fantasy. Emma checked her watch and grinned. It was 8:30 in the morning.

She found the apartment and rang the doorbell. Waited. Rang. Waited. Rang. Fantasy finally opened the door wearing a pink fuzzy robe and matching bunny slippers. They both blinked at each other several times.

Bunny slippers? Emma thought.

Fantasy looked as if she were going to a Halloween party as a zombie. Her long, white-bleached hair was tangled and mascara circled her eyes. She yawned as she examined Emma, who wore her normal attire of khaki shorts, Keen sandals, and a *Life Is Good* T-shirt. This one sported the infamous, smiling, stick man, waving as he was kayaking. She was damp from the rain but figured she had to look better than Fantasy.

"Hello," Emma said.

"Who are you and what do you want?" Fantasy asked.

"Are you Fae Vernon?" Emma asked.

Fantasy yawned again. "Who are you and what do you want?" she repeated, louder this time.

"My name is Emma Haines. I'm a friend of Joey Reed."

Fantasy's eyes grew wide, and she was suddenly awake.

"Don't worry," Emma said, holding up her hands like she was surrendering. "I come in peace. He just wanted me to ask you a few questions that might help an investigation." Emma looked her over again. She couldn't see what Joey and Merek saw in this woman. But then again, she could surmise.

"*Investigation?* What are you talking about? Are you with the police?"

"No. I'm a friend."

"Wait a minute. Emma Haines. I know who you are. You're Merek's boss."

"I'm not his boss. I'm his partner."

She looked confused. "Yeah, whatever. What do you want? How do you know Joey? What is this about? Where's Joey?"

"Joey couldn't make it."

"What's this about?"

"May I come in?" Emma asked.

The two women stood, measuring each other. Fantasy finally motioned with her chin for Emma to come in and opened the door wider. Emma followed Fantasy into a large open living and kitchen area.

"I need coffee. You want some?" Fantasy asked over her shoulder as she scuffed into the kitchen in her bunny slippers.

"Sure. Sounds good." Emma looked around. "Really nice place you've got here."

Fantasy didn't reply as she puttered around the sleek kitchen, complete with Bosch appliances and granite countertops. A large palm-leaf ceiling fan twirled above them.

"You dating Joey? Is that why you're here? Cause if that's the reason …"

Emma laughed, interrupting her. "Joey Reed and I have worked together for a long time, and the thought of dating each other has never come into the picture. Our relationship is strictly professional."

Fantasy frowned at her. "When did you work with him?"

"He was my main contact on the police force when I worked at Matrix Insurance as a fraud investigator a long time ago. We became good friends, but that's all."

"I'll bet," Fantasy said with a smirk.

"It's nothing like that. It's much bigger than that, Fantasy."

"What's that supposed to mean? Where is he, anyway?"

"You don't know?"

"No. Why would I know? I haven't seen Joey in a long time. And I don't really care where he is. That's the truth, I swear. I hate him."

"Hate? That's a pretty strong word. When *is* the last time you saw him?" Emma asked."

"That's none of your business."

"Fantasy, where were you on Saturday?"

"I was here. Then I went to work. Why do you want to know? Why's it any of your business?"

"Can anyone back you up on that?" Emma asked.

"Why? What's this about anyway? I thought you said you're not a cop. You need to leave." Her voice was rising, and she fumbled with the coffee maker. Either she was hiding something or she still had strong feelings for Joey Reed—or both.

Emma looked at her for a long time. "Fantasy, Joey was in a serious boating accident Saturday. He was nearly killed."

Her mouth fell open. She shut it quickly and tried to look aloof. "Good. Like I said, I hate him." She turned away as her eyes filled with tears. "What happened?" she asked, her back to Emma.

Emma told her without going into details. "I thought you might have seen it on the news or in the paper," she added.

Fantasy poured coffee into the cups, turned, and handed one to Emma with a shaking hand before pushing a sugar bowl toward her. "You need milk?" she squeaked.

Emma shook her head. "I like it black." She took a sip, as if to prove the point.

Fantasy poured several teaspoons of sugar and milk into her coffee, sipped it, then raised and tilted her head. "You think I had something to do with that? I sure don't have a boat, if that's what this is about. I don't have anything to do with any of that." She waved a silver sparkling fingernail toward Emma. "I think you need to leave before I call the cops."

Emma shrugged and put the cup on the counter. "That's fine. I'll go. But if you can think of anything that might help us out about this, call me. Don't call Joey. He's in the hospital and can't accept any calls or have visitors right now."

Emma stood and pulled a business card from her purse and placed it on the counter. "It was a terrible accident, and I'm talking to everyone who knows him."

"You mean anyone that might hate him."

"I'd be careful using that word right now," Emma said with a sideways glance.

Fantasy shrugged. "I don't care. I do hate him. He hurt me. He hurt me bad. But I would never hurt him. Besides, like I said, I don't have a boat." Fantasy lifted her head. "And I couldn't hurt anyone. I'm just not like that. I'm a lover, not a fighter. No matter what."

She reached over and snatched up the card. Her heart did another flip when she saw Merek's name on it before the word "Partner" and the familiar cell number. She shoved it into her robe pocket when she realized how much her hand was shaking.

"Look, Fantasy. No matter what happened between you and Joey, he could use your help right now." Emma's eyes swept over the kitchen.

Fantasy blew on her coffee and eyed Emma over the brim of the cup.

Emma walked closer toward her so she could get a better look at a calendar hanging on the refrigerator over Fantasy's shoulder. She squinted, trying to read what was scribbled in Saturday's box before she looked back into Fantasy's raccoon-ringed eyes. Fantasy came rushing toward her. "You need to go. Right now! Get out!" She yelled, pointing toward the door.

Emma let herself out, leaving Fantasy in her pink robe and bunny slippers.

As soon as the door shut behind Emma, Fantasy ran

into her bedroom and grabbed the cell phone that Brexton had bought for her from the bedside table. She nearly dropped it as she took a deep breath and hit a number in the *Favorites* she never called before, only texted. She paced the condo and walked back into the living room, continuing to walk in circles.

Brexton Birch answered in a low voice, "Why are you calling me? I thought we agreed you would never call."

"I know. I'm sorry, but I had to. You need to know that a woman was just here. She's a friend of Joey's. She wants to know where I was Saturday because of his accident."

"Who? What? Slow down. What are you talking about?" Brexton asked.

She explained Emma's visit, having to back up and start over several times.

"You didn't tell her about the video or mention anything about me, did you?"

"No. I wouldn't do that. But Brexton, honey, you need to tell the police and show them that movie you got with your helicopter toy. That's got to be what she's talking about. It's that accident. It's Joey on that video. I can't believe it. But it's got to be her and Joey in those little tiny boats and—"

He interrupted her. "I was afraid of that when I saw the paper yesterday morning. We discussed this. Remember? We do not have a video of any kind, and we know nothing about a boating accident, and you do not *even know me*. No matter what. You know this," Brexton replied, trying to retain his composure.

"Yeah, I know. I know, honey. But it's all just so weird. That's Joey on that video getting run over by that boat. It's got to be. You've got to help them find that boat driver."

"Absolutely not. Do you understand that our relationship depends on you never mentioning anything about Saturday or me—*ever*—to anyone at all? No matter what. Do I make myself clear, Fantasy? Because if you do—we're through. Period. No more condo or car or presents or boat rides ... or me. Understand?"

"Yes, yes, sweetheart. I understand. But I'm afraid, is all. What if the police come here asking me questions again? Joey *is* a cop, you know." She nearly dropped the cell again.

"I'm aware of that. You've told me about him much too often. As a matter of fact, I wonder if you really love me, Fantasy. Maybe you still love him," Brexton said in an accusatory voice.

"No, I don't. No. I don't! You know I love you. He just hurt me so bad, is all. I'm sorry. I won't talk about him anymore." She began to cry. "I love you, Brexton. I love you. I love *you*."

Silence.

"Then you will never talk about Saturday or me to anyone. Agreed?"

Fantasy nodded.

"Agreed?" Brexton nearly screamed into the phone before he glanced around his office. "Now, calm down and tell me exactly, word-for-word, what you told this Emma woman."

She told him.

"You told her you were at *work*?"

"It's the first thing that popped into my head. You've got to understand. I was so upset and nervous when I realized that movie you showed me was Joey getting run over."

"That was certainly ignorant of you. So terribly stupid," he said.

"Why?"

"Think about it, Fantasy." He stomped his foot and made a fist with his free hand and banged it on his desk.

Fantasy squeezed her eyes. "I'm sorry. I'm sorry. I love you, Brexton. Please, don't be mad at me. I'll do anything for you. Please …" she trailed off, sobbing.

Brexton closed his eyes. "Listen. Just go about your day. Act normal and this will all simply go away. She's not with the police. She'll find something better to do. Don't worry about any of this. I'll fix everything."

"Okay. I knew you would, honey." Fantasy smiled and choked out, "I love you."

"Yes, I'm well aware of that. Now listen to me. No matter what, do not talk to anyone about this. I'll be in touch." He ended the call. "Stupid slut," he whispered. He stood, slipped the cell in his inside jacket pocket, buttoned his jacket, straightened his tie, and hurried down the wood-paneled hallway. He took a deep breath before he entered the conference room.

"Apologies for being late. My wife is a bit under the weather and I asked her to let me know if there was anything I could bring home for her. She's been working long hours lately, volunteering at the children's hospital, and she's caught a little bug. I'm sure you understand," he said as he sat down in a black leather chair at the head of the conference table and opened a folder. "So, we're here to discuss your million-dollar, monthly alimony payment. I agree. I don't think it's enough either." He smiled and leaned back in his chair.

***

Emma was in her truck. She looked at the door of Brown's Steakhouse. It didn't open until eleven, but she was driving by on her way from Fantasy's and thought it might save her a trip later.

She had eaten here several times with Stratton. It was the poshest restaurant in town, and the steaks were worth every cent. She got out of her truck and walked beneath the green awning. She peered through the locked, glass door. She saw movement and tapped on the door.

A young man came to the door, dressed in a brown janitor uniform. He shook his head and pointed to the gold embossed hours displayed on the door. Emma said loudly, "I know. But I need to talk to the manager, if he's in." She gave her best smile.

The janitor unlocked the door and stuck his head outside. "He is in his office, but he is busy, and we're not open yet."

"I know. And I'm sorry. But this is really important. It's about a police investigation."

The man looked surprised. "Wait here." He locked the door again.

He returned, unlocked the door, and led her through the restaurant to an open door with red letters that read "Private."

A young man stood, smiled, and came around the desk, extending his hand to her. "Aaron Wells. Are you a police officer?" He looked at her, questioningly.

"No. But this is about a police investigation. My name is Emma Haines. Thanks for seeing me." She shook his hand. "I'm helping a friend of mine, who is a police officer. He's in the hospital. He was in a boating accident on Saturday. I'm asking a few questions around town for him."

The man put his hands in his pockets and gave her a puzzled look. "Oh, yes. I saw it on the news. I remember now. You were with him."

"Yes," she said.

"I'm sorry about your friend. How can I help you?"

"Do you do the employee scheduling?" she asked.

"Yes. Why?"

"Could you tell me when one of your waitresses works here? Her name is Fae Vernon. I need to talk to her about the case, but I'm not sure where she lives, so I thought I could catch her here."

The man took a deep breath and shook his head. "I'm sorry, I can't give out that kind of information unless you have a warrant and you're an officer of the law. Privacy. You understand."

"I do. But I thought it would save me some time," she said.

He looked at her again. She returned the look.

"What's Ms. Vernon got to do with this?"

"Nothing, I'm sure. I'm just asking people questions who know Joey. You know, trying to connect dots. She may know someone who knows someone. That sort of thing."

"Sounded like a bad accident."

"Yes. That's what it looks like," Emma said.

"Looks like?" The man's eyebrows rose. "You don't think it was an accident?"

"I don't think anything. All I know is he was plowed over by a speedboat right in front of me and I'm trying to help him find out who was driving it. Insurance. He's going to have major hospital bills, and he shouldn't have to pay for them. I'm just trying to help him. That's all."

"I see. You don't think *Ms. Vernon* ran over him in a boat, do you?" he said, half-smiling.

"No. But maybe she knows someone who may know someone. That's all. That's just how investigations work. I'm a former insurance fraud investigator. That's how I met Joey. He and I solved many cases together." She got a card out of her purse and handed it to him, telling him more about herself and her history with Joey.

He rocked back on his heels as he examined it. "Why aren't the police here doing this?"

"They will be. Joey and I go way back. I'm just trying to help, too. That's all."

He walked over to his desk and sat down. He looked at Emma for a long moment and then clicked the computer mouse. His eyes glanced over the screen as he clicked the mouse and tapped the keyboard.

"She'll be here again tomorrow. She works lunch shift to dinner, Tuesdays through Friday. She comes in around ten thirty."

"She doesn't work on the weekends?"

"No. She used to. But she has the weekends and Mondays off. She switched with another worker. I believe her mother is ill, and she spends the weekends with her. We don't like turnover here at Brown's. We pay our staff well and keep them happy by being flexible. That's one reason why we have the best customer service in the business," he said proudly.

"That's very nice of you to work with her like that. It's too bad about her mother. Is she terminal?"

The man scowled. "I've already told you more than I should have. Now, if you'll excuse me, I have work to do."

"Certainly. Thank you for your time. You know, I've eaten here. The service and food were great," Emma said.

"Thank you. I'll be checking up on you, you know. And I'll report you to the police if I find out your story isn't true."

"I expect nothing less. You can call Joey's boss, the chief of police. He knows me."

"You can count on it."

"Thank you again, Mr. Wells."

"I'll do anything to help a police officer."

Emma left Brown's and sat in her truck. "You are such a dipshit liar," she said, turning the truck back toward Fantasy's apartment. She would confront her head-on, keep her there, call the police, and be done with it. Case closed.

Twenty minutes later she stood at Fantasy's door again, but there was no answer after several doorbell buzzes and knocks. Emma walked back to the truck and got in. It was around noon and her stomach was growling.

***

Emma tapped on Joey's hospital room door and held up two bags from McDonald's. "Special delivery," she said.

"Great! Bring it on in here," Joey said. "I'm hungry."

She walked in, arranged the food on the rolling table and moved it above Joey's chest. He dived into the fries as Emma pulled the chair next to his bed and sat down.

She started telling him about her day. "Anyway, I think Fantasy may be involved with this. There was a note on her calendar that read, 'Boat Ride.' It was written on Saturday, but she told me she was at work on Saturday. I went to Brown's, and she wasn't at work on Saturday. She doesn't work on Saturdays. She lied."

Joey stopped mid-chew. "What the ..." He shook his head. "Are you sure? That's even too stupid for her to lie about," he mumbled through chewing. He washed his food down with a swig of his drink.

"Obviously not," she said.

"She wrote it on her calendar? Why would she do that and lie about being at work? Wouldn't she know how easy it is to check all this?" he said.

"You know her, not me. She was nervous when I talked to her. Her hands were shaking and she made little eye contact. I think being at work was the first thing that fell out of that pretty little mouth of hers. And as soon as I left, I stuck my ear to the door and heard movement, mumbling, probably on her cell. I couldn't make out what she was saying, but I could hear her voice rising and falling and I could've sworn she was crying.

"She's definitely covering something up, Joey. And, to each their own, but she doesn't strike me as the sharpest knife in the drawer." She took a bite of her Big Mac, chewed, and swallowed. "And the big bad thing is, if she hates you as much as she said she does, and she did try to have you killed—she knows you're still alive and might try to finish what she started."

As Emma and Joey ate their lunch, there was a tap on the door. An officer in uniform stood in the doorway.

"Matt, come on in, guy. Great to see you," Joey said, motioning for the man to come in.

"You sure? I can come back. Looks like you're busy."

"No, no. Come on in. This is my friend Emma Haines. She's a former insurance fraud investigator turned consultant. She and I go back a long way. You don't mind, do you, Emma?"

She shook her head, swallowed, wiped her hands on a napkin, and stood. "Nice to meet you, Matt. Please, join us." He removed his hat, and they shook hands. She pulled another chair next to Joey's bed.

"You sure it's okay? I don't want to interrupt anything," he said, glancing back and forth between them.

"You're not interrupting anything at all. Joey and I were just discussing who might have done this to him. Please, sit down."

He looked Joey over. "Wow. You really got busted up, didn't you?"

Joey nodded, shoving the last fry into his mouth.

"He's lucky," Emma said, cleaning up their lunch wrappers and shoving them into the bags.

Joey looked at her. "Easy for you to say." He turned to Matt. "They want to keep me for observation. See what's going on inside me."

"Do you have any leads?" Matt asked.

Joey and Emma glanced at each other. Emma looked away and Joey said, "No. I doubt we'll ever find out who it was. Just a crazy accident." Joey looked down at himself. "Can you believe this?" he laughed.

"It's a bum deal, for sure. But you're going to be okay?" Matta asked.

"Yeah. It'll just take time to heal. They told me the breaks were clean. No major problems there."

"The news said it was a white boat with a windshield and dark Bimini?" Matt asked.

"Yes. I was too far away to see much else, but I could see that much," Emma said.

"Man, I'm really sorry about this. Anything we can

do at the station, just let us know. I know everyone will be stopping in when they can."

"I can tell you right now, once I get home, I'm going to need beer deliveries," Joey said with a lopsided grin.

"Not a problem, my friend," Matt said, smiling.

"So, how long have you been a cop?" Emma asked.

"Going on five years or so. I went to the academy when I returned from Iraq."

"Matt here can shoot the balls off a mouse from a mile away," Joey said.

"I see," Emma smiled.

"Joey ..." Matt said, surprised.

"It's okay. She knows all about snipers." He went on to explain their history together.

Emma held up a hand. "Your secret's safe with me. No problem. I've always been fascinated by guys like you. I can't even hold a gun, let alone hit anything with one."

"I've tried to get her to go to the firing range, but she's never found the time," Joey said. "She should carry, as far as I'm concerned."

***

Emma drove east on North Broadway toward her condo. Her mind was restless. She had stayed at the hospital for several hours and then run a few errands while thinking about the case. *Could Fantasy have done this? Really? What an airhead.* Her thoughts shifted to Stratton.

Stratton had twenty years on Emma's forty-seven, but he was in great shape, sharp, and handsome. They had been through a lot together, and she loved him. Before he left on this book tour in Europe, they both knew they needed time apart. Things had turned weird—downright ugly for a few weeks, even. He'd been living with her at her Clintonville condo for over a year, but she asked him to go to his home in West Virginia. Then he called and said his publisher had lined up a six-month book tour in Europe. She went over with him and stayed for a couple of weeks, but came home and wished him well.

She sat at the stoplight staring blankly at the traffic passing in front of her on High Street. She wondered when the law passed that everyone had to be talking on a cellphone while driving. *Silly human race*, for sure, thinking of a lyric of Jon Anderson's, the former lead singer of her favorite rock band, YES.

The light turned and she made a left onto High Street, passing the Whetstone Library. She remembered that she needed to pick up books that were on hold.

She made a right onto her street and pulled the truck into the garage. As she got out, she smiled as Millie howled and barked—Emma's welcome-home song.

Emma walked toward the window and waved at the dog. Millie was standing on the back of the love seat looking at Emma through the window, howling and wagging her tail. Emma could hear the dog's tail thumping the wall.

"Hi, baby girl. Mommy's home. Want to go for a walk?"

Millie barked. When Emma got into the kitchen, Millie howled, jumped on her, and bounced around her feet, her long ears flopping in all directions.

"No matter what, you're always glad to see me. And I'm always glad to see you, too." She bent to pet and hug the dog. She got Millie's harness, fastened it, and hooked the leash. "Let's go."

They trotted down the steps and walked down the block. Emma proceeded to tell Millie about her day as the dog squatted to pee. They continued to walk as Millie sniffed the ground along the way, wagging her tail and occasionally glancing up at Emma as if she were somewhat interested in the conversation.

Emma smiled as she watched Millie answer another pee-mail. When they turned the corner, Emma's cell rang.

She read the screen. "Ahhh, gheesh. I am not in the mood to talk to *him*." She rolled her eyes as she slid the *Accept Call* icon on her iPhone. "Hey, Calvin. What's up?"

"Emma. I'm surprised you answered. I was just going to leave you a message."

She didn't reply.

"Are you there?" he said, clearly annoyed.

"Yeah, I'm here. What's up?"

"I need more changes to the presentation."

"Calvin, I ..." She stopped. "Actually, I'm glad you called. I was going to call you tomorrow."

"You were?" he asked, surprised.

"Yeah. I need you to check C.L.U.E. for me and keep an eye on it to see if any claims come through on a damaged white speedboat from around the O'Shaughnessy Reservoir area."

"Oh, yes. Joey Reed's accident. I heard about it," Calvin said. "Damn shame. He's a good cop."

"Yes, he is. Anyway, there might have been some damage to the boat that hit the kayak. I doubt it, but never hurts to monitor any claims that come in. When can you check it out?"

"Hold on, little lady. I don't work for you. You work for me. And don't' ever forget it. You and that idiot office manager of yours."

"Merek is not an idiot. He's a genius. And he does great work. You know that. And he's not my office manager, he's my partner."

"Yeah, yeah. Whatever. I still don't like the tattooed, pierced Pole. He's shifty."

Emma held back a snort. Calvin Nelson was one of the biggest scoundrels she'd ever met. But he knew about insurance claims and Mr. Matrix, the elderly owner of Matrix Insurance, worshiped him.

"Tell you what, Emma. We'll trade my changes for your information. And I'll only start trading over lunch at my place, starting tomorrow."

Emma let the words roll off her back as usual, while she watched Millie, who was sniffing the base of a tree.

Calvin had been in love with her since she started working at Matrix Insurance over two decades ago. He cooled off after—she suspected—Stratton had a talk with him. But Calvin knew Stratton was in Europe and turned up the heat yet again.

Calvin was *almost* five feet tall, with huge feet, and a bad white hair-plug job that made him look like he had a plastic white scrubber on his head. He reminded Emma of Humpty Dumpty. But he pulled the main purse strings at H.I.T. and he, Merek, and Emma knew it. It was a stressful business relationship, but the money allowed Emma and Merek to live the way they liked. Everything has a price.

"Okay. Deal. What time?" she said.

Calvin said nothing.

"You there?" she asked, grinning.

"Yes. Yes, I'm here. Okay, then. Around one. You be at my place at one tomorrow," he said.

"Not surprisingly, I don't know where you live."

He rattled off the address.

"I don't have anything to write with and I may not remember," she said. "I'm walking my dog."

"Just call my new secretary in the morning—can't remember this one's name, either—she'll give it to you. Be there at one. Sharp." He ended the call.

"Merek will see you at one, Calvin," she said to the blank screen.

Millie glanced up at Emma and wagged her white-tipped tail as they continued their walk.

***

Monday afternoon, Emma and Merek sat at the small conference table in H.I.T.'s office. Emma faced the soles of Merek's biker boots propped on a chair as she talked on her iPhone.

"Yeah. Right. Okay." She glanced at Merek. "Right. I'll be around later. Bye." She hit the end call icon and laid her iPhone on the table.

"Mr. Joey?"

"Yeah." She paused. "I met Fantasy yesterday."

Merek frowned and squinted.

"Don't worry. Your name wasn't in the script. I just have to say ... I don't understand how smart guys like you and Joey get involved with chicks like her and Ludnella."

Merek once loved a long-legged, bleach-blonde woman named Ludnella Czerwinski. He flew to Colorado to save her from a bad marriage and bring her back to Clintonville. Just before he kicked the shit out of her husband in self-defense, she informed Merek she was pregnant by her husband. He offered to bring her to Clintonville and raise the child as his own. But she stayed with her husband.

"You know a lot of it, Miss H.," he mumbled.

"Yeah, I do. But a stripper?"

"A beautiful woman. Giving and caring. But possessive. She just wants to settle down and have a family, like most women."

Emma didn't know if that was a jab but ignored it. Stratton was anything but possessive, but he had become fatherly and bossy. It probably didn't help that she was the same age as his daughter, Ellen and a year older than his son, Glen.

"I get it. I do. We fall in love and then …" she trailed off. "Speaking of love, guess who you're going to have lunch with." She brightened.

Merek looked confused, raising his palms to the ceiling and shrugging.

"Our buddy, Calvin Nelson."

"Ja pierdziele!"

"Yeah. Whatever. Anyway, he thinks that *I'm* coming over for lunch tomorrow," she made quotations in the air with her fingers. "He wants even more changes to the last presentation. I want him to monitor the claims system and see if anyone files a boat damage claim that could be connected to Joey's accident. Whoever hit Joey might have been dumb enough to file a claim. You never know. They could claim they hit a log or something. Calvin said we would make an information trade," she said.

"It is not his presentation he is interested in, Miss H."

"Ya think?"

They laughed.

"I wish I could be there to see the look on his face when he opens the door and sees you. Just so you know, Calvin's a pretty prejudice jerk, if you get my drift."

Merek shrugged. "He does not like me. I already know this. And I do not care."

"I know. Just don't hurt him. And make him feed you. He'll probably whip up a fine meal.

"I'm heading over to the park service office now and look through video tapes of Saturday morning. Maybe someone trailered that boat there and parked in one of the public lots around the lake. They've all got surveillance cameras. Maybe I'll see *something*," she said.

"How many lots?" Merek asked.

"Three," she answered.

"That is quite a shot long," he said.

She grinned. "Yeah. It's a long shot, but at least I've got to try. And Fantasy is lying to me about where she was Saturday. She known to stretch the truth a little?"

"She lies, Miss H.*"*

"Everyone does when they have to. Anyway, I was wondering if you think she'd talk to you. She made it clear, she doesn't want to talk to me. Or looking at her calendar on her fridge."

They looked at each other for a long moment.

"I will go talk to her," he said.

"I think you need to do more than talk to her. You need to do a little surveillance."

***

"See anything?" Toby, the park ranger, asked Emma.

She shook her head and yawned. "No. Just a few

fishermen come in and unload, but not the boat I saw." She checked her watch. "This is a waste of time."

"If you didn't see anything, it wasn't a waste of time. You're probably looking for someone who lives along the lake. But that could be dozens of people from miles upstream to right above the dam. And lots of people have boats all over the area that bring them here and launch them from other places. And I have to be honest with you, Ms. Haines. There's a lot of boats like you described."

"Okay. I get that, but that's all I remember. Everything happened so fast. I wish I could remember more."

"I'm sorry about your friend. He going to recover?"

"Yes, thank goodness. That boat plowed right over him. I figure the kayak turned over and Joey got pushed under the water and out of the way. He's got a broken arm and leg, a concussion, cracked ribs, bumps and bruises. It could've been much worse."

Toby shook his head. "What a crazy accident. I think the driver freaked out and fled the scene."

"I hope to find out. Hey, thanks for pulling these for me. I'm heading home."

"No problem. I'll keep an eye out for your hit-and-run driver."

"Sounds good."

***

Emma sat on Mary Wellington's sun porch and watched the western sky turn pink over her 18-hole golf course on the Wellington Estate near Circleville, Ohio. Emma was close friends with Mary's son, Charles Wellington III.

They met twenty-three years ago while riding their bicycles to work on the Olentangy Bike Path in opposite directions. They discovered they loved the outdoors, and Emma turned Charles on to kayaking. They'd gone kayaking almost every weekend since until Charles took a transfer from the engineering firm, Bridge Systems in Clintonville, Ohio, to its office in Switzerland two years ago.

Mary Wellington held the title of the world's best senior woman golfer. She traveled the globe, winning tournaments. The proof was on display in her trophy room off the library. She was also featured in sports magazines and tabloids. Even at her age, Mary had an active dating reputation and the media loved it. So did she.

"More wine?" John, Mary's butler and cook, asked Emma. His silver hair shined in the evening light. He wore a black vest over his white, high-collared, button-down shirt, under a black blazer.

Emma smiled and shook her head. "No, thank you, John. I'm good. How've you been?"

John started to answer but was interrupted by Mary who blurted, "Oh, don't be ridiculous, dear. You can spend the night. Drink up. I get tired of drinking alone." She sipped her second martini.

John gave Emma a wide-eyed look, glancing at Mary. "I've been ... busy, thank you." He left the room. Emma watched him walk away before she turned back to Mary.

"No, thanks. I've got an assignment, and I need a clear head tomorrow."

Mary waved a red-polished, manicured, wrinkled hand. "A clear head. Whatever that means. What is this new assignment? Can you tell me? Or is it a big secret?" Secret came out "sheeehkret," along with a bit of spittle.

Emma thought about it before answering. "I don't see why not. Maybe you can give me a different perspective."

"Splendid. Do tell."

"I don't know if you heard about my friend Joey Reed …"

"Oh, yes! How awful. The officer who helped me put Devereux away. Emma, I must admit, my first thought was I was glad it wasn't Charles. I'm sorry dear, and you know I love you like my own daughter, but he's my only son and you've put him in a couple of very dangerous situations with that canoeing you two do." She took another drink.

Emma's ears turned warm. She certainly didn't need Mary Wellington's load right now.

"Oh, don't you worry. I never blamed you. Truly. I just, well, he is my only child and having mere criminals shoot at him. And you are the one that introduced him to it all. But I've never blamed you for his love of canoeing."

"Kayaking," Emma said softly.

"Whatever it is. Those little plastic boats out there on the water. Anyway. I do believe you saved him from having a major breakdown after Simon left him with that kayaking and all. And I'll always be grateful to you for that."

Oh, Mary. You have no idea, Emma thought as she took a sip of wine.

Simon and Charles had been partners for over twenty years, but without any warning, Simon walked out to move to Spain. Two years ago, Simon Johnson's body had been found outside Columbus. After Dayton

Kotmister kidnapped Stratton, Kotmister's hit man confessed to shooting Simon. Kotmister wanted to date Charles, but Charles ignored him. To get back at Charles, Kotmister ordered Simon to move to Spain or he'd kill Charles. Sadly, Simon ended up paying with his life.

"And that skunk, Devereux. I hope he rots in prison. I still cannot believe I fell for him. How could I have been such a fool?" She pounded a fist on the table.

"We all make mistakes in the name of love," Emma said.

Mary patted Emma's arm. "You're preaching to the choir, my dear. But you. You're different. You have Stratton Reeves. He's quite a catch," she slurred and winked crookedly at Emma.

Emma looked down at the table but said nothing. Years ago, at one of Mary's parties, her flirting with Stratton turned into nothing but entertainment for Emma and Stratton and the usual embarrassment for Charles.

"I'm sorry. Go ahead." She turned and raised her glass toward the one-way mirrored wall that separated the sun porch from the kitchen. Within seconds, John was at her side, filling her glass from the martini pitcher and plopping fresh-speared olives into it before he left.

"Mary, are you okay?"

"Okay? What do you mean, dear?"

Emma gazed at Mary's martini glass.

"I suppose you think I'm a drunk, too?"

"I didn't say that. Drinking is fine in moderation. It's just …"

"It's just that you've been talking to Charles and he's concerned about his seventy-nine-year-old drunk mother. If he's that damned concerned, why is he living alone in Switzerland? Why hasn't he asked me to move there and live with him? Or at least visit him? I always hear he's too busy or he's coming back here to visit. That he cannot wait to see me and stay here a few days and ..." she trailed off in a slur, taking another swig of her drink. "I even offered to go there several times, but he doesn't have time for me. It's like he doesn't want me there."

Emma wasn't about to break the news that Charles had taken his father with him to Switzerland and they'd been living together for the past two years in a lakeside mansion at the foot of snow-topped mountains. The view from Charles's home was surreal. Mary would flip and even disown him if she knew Charles had befriended his father. Mary had sent Charles's father packing, or at least she thought so, when he showed up on her doorstep unannounced a few years ago. But Charles had a soft heart, like his father, and took him under his wing and provided for him. No one ever breathed a word of it to Mary.

"He's just busy with his job."

"Oh, his job. His job. His job. He doesn't need that job. Have you visited him?" Mary asked.

Emma couldn't answer. She didn't want to lie to Mary, but she didn't want to tell her she and Stratton had visited Charles and his father twice since they'd moved.

She grabbed her purse. "Excuse me. I have to take this call." She stood and pulled her phone from her purse.

Mary looked puzzled as Emma walked out of the sunroom with her phone to her ear. She put the phone back in her purse when she was out of Mary's sight.

Tuesday

MEREK SAT AT the counter in the Wildflower Café, eating steak and eggs for breakfast. Autumn, a waitress, poured more coffee into his mug. "I was surprised when you moved back from Poland. I thought you moved there to live with your family," she said.

"It was my plan, but I belong here now. I may return someday."

"Cool. There's nothing like family. You working for Emma again?"

"She made me partner of the business before I left." He beamed. "It is good."

Autumn nodded and smiled. "Emma's nice. She was in here a couple of weeks ago for lunch. Sat in the corner reading."

He sipped his coffee. "Have you seen Fantasy in here lately?"

"Fantasy? Not for a long time, maybe a few months. Last time I saw her in here, she was with that cop Joey Reed. Oh, I'm sorry. Maybe I shouldn't have told you that."

"It is fine. I know about them. Fantasy and I split up

before I went to Poland. It is no problem. I just wondered if you had seen her in here lately."

"No. Like I said, it's been awhile." She paused. "So are you seeing anyone?"

Merek shrugged and looked at the counter. He knew Autumn was aware of his reputation as a "dater," and that she had an eye for him. "No. But I have strong feelings for someone who lives far away. I cannot date."

Autumn looked puzzled. "Yeah? Another blonde bombshell, I suppose. Long-distance relationships are usually a pain, but I guess some work out. I get it." She shrugged and looked away.

"I am glad you do because I do not. I have not seen this woman in over two years, and I only met her once for about thirty minutes. She has black hair. She has been on my mind since."

"Wow! She must be some woman. And not even blonde. That is a big switch for you."

He nodded.

"Where'd you meet her?"

"Kentucky, two years ago. I stopped in an old store and she was there. It was her parents' store. She was cleaning it out after they died. She lives in New York City. But we have, what is it? Reconnected? Yes. Reconnected." He sipped his coffee before he continued. "I did not date when I was in Poland. My mother always says to me, 'You are almost thirty years old. Will you never give me grandchildren?'"

"Yeah, I used to hear that. Then I married a jerk. It didn't last long. But the good thing out of it was my daughter. And he is a great dad. Now, I don't get asked that anymore." She shrugged. "We all love her. She's spoiled."

Merek wiped his mouth with the napkin. "That is good."

"Yeah." Customers came in the door and stood, waiting to be seated. "You ready for your check?" she asked.

"Yes, please."

She ripped it off her pad and laid it in front of him before she seated the new arrivals.

Merek went to the register. Autumn swiped his credit card through the Apple register and turned the screen toward him. He added a forty percent tip and scribbled his name with his finger.

"Take care, Merek. Good to see you again. Come back soon," Autumn said.

"You will see me often, just like before," he said.

"I'm glad," she said, smiling.

Merek strolled outside to his Harley. He put on his gloves and helmet, threw his leg over the seat, and started the engine.

He had forgotten how much he missed riding it. He sold his bike before he moved to Poland. When he returned, he called the man who bought it to see if he could buy it back. The man said he didn't have as much time to ride as he expected. He added, "I only rode it once, and my wife hates it. She told me I have to sell it." He sold it back to Merek for the same price he paid for it. Both men were pleased.

Merek pulled onto Indianola Avenue and headed toward Fantasy's condo. It was his turn to ask the questions.

***

Emma sat in her kayak and surveyed the area where Joey was run over four days ago, trying to re-create the scene in her mind. But like all memories, it had faded with time and uncertainty had crept in. Still, she had to try.

She looked toward where the speedboat first appeared. She remembered the sound of the engine and the punch in her stomach. She hadn't told Joey about looking for boats because she hadn't planned on taking him out on the open reservoir. She was going to stay along the edges and in the small coves since it was his first time kayaking.

She pictured the speeding boat. That's when she started yelling and screaming. She had paddled hard chasing him, but he was too far away.

Her memories were interrupted by a drone that moved back and forth above the tree line, along the shore. Up and down. Out over the water. Back toward the shore.

She'd been reading about drones and their possible uses in claims investigations for roof inspections and after catastrophes when adjusters had a hard time getting to an area because of the devastation and possible safety hazards. She had put a few slides about them in her latest presentation for Calvin.

She paddled toward the bank and looked for the operator. The drone started to descend, and she made out the silhouettes of two people, a taller one and a shorter one. She paddled closer to an older man and a young boy who landed the drone. The drone's propellers stopped, and it sat at their feet.

"Hey, there," she waved and paddled closer.

"I'm sorry. Did our drone scare you?" the man asked.

"No, I was just curious and followed it."

"I apologize if it frightened you. This is my grandson's science project. We're using it to take pictures of the lake." The man looked down at the boy with pride.

"No, it didn't scare me. I'm not that familiar with them. I've only been reading about them for use in my line of business."

"What kind of work do you do?"

"I work in insurance claims as a trainer."

"Oh, why yes. Makes perfect sense. Bobby's project is about this reservoir. We're having fun working on it together. I'm learning more than he is."

"That's great. There's a camera mounted on your drone, right?"

"Yes. I'm taking pictures of the lake and writing a report about the history and how we can all help keep it clean for the future."

Emma smiled. "I'm all for that. Sounds like a cool project."

The boy walked closer to the water. "It is." He paused, examining Emma's boat. "That's a neat kayak."

"You know about kayaks?"

"Me and my dad have one, and we take it fishing sometimes. We watch sunsets and birds, too." He turned to his grandfather. "Hey, Grandpa, maybe Dad and I could take the drone out in the boat for my project."

"That's a great idea. We'll need to check the rules first, but let's talk to your dad when we get back." The boy turned to Emma.

She said, "I like to watch sunsets and birds from my kayak, too. My kayak's name is *Arlene*, named after a friend of mine."

The boy laughed. "You named your kayak?"

"Doesn't surprise me," the man said. "Many boats have a lady's name."

"Why?" the boy asked, looking at his grandfather.

"I think that's another good thing for *you* to look into," the man said.

"Okay," Bobby said, picking up the drone.

"My name's Emma."

"My name is Chester, and as you know, this is Bobby."

"Pleased to meet you both," Emma said, glancing at the sky. "You wouldn't have happened to have been out here around seven in the morning on Saturday with your drone, would you?"

***

Joey pointed the remote at the TV and flipped through the channels. He turned it off and laid the remote on the bed. He glanced at the stack of books and magazines on the side table. Nothing looked good.

"I'm freaking out already and I've only been in here for four days," he said aloud. I just have to stay calm. I'll heal, and everything will be fine."

He laid his head deep in the pillow. His mind wandered down a path he didn't really want it to go. After all the relationships he'd had, here he was, alone, waiting on his next friend or relative to find time in their lives to wander into this ugly room to spend a few minutes with him. Most of them had better things to do.

I'm pushing fifty, but at least I don't have ex-wives and I'm not in debt with child support or alimony payments. I'm a free man. I can come and go as I please and date whomever I want. And I'm good at my job, which gets in the way of a relationship. No one to answer to. He volleyed these thoughts in his head often.

"At least I don't have to worry about that," he said aloud.

"Worry about what?" a voice asked.

He turned his head to see Sheriff Leila Day, smiling. She was in full uniform, and her head nearly reached the top of the of the doorway.

"Is this a bad time?" she asked.

"Leila, hello. No, no. Come in. It's great to see you. Come in, have a seat," he said as he pushed the button to raise the bed. "You just caught me talking to myself."

She walked into the room, filling it with her thin, six-foot-two-inch frame. "Are you sure? I can come back. Unfortunately, it looks like you may not be going very far for a while."

"Yeah. The nurses here wanted to make sure of that. They just did this to keep me here. Come on in and have a seat."

"Some things never change. These orange plastic chairs always look inviting," she said, moving the chair closer to his bedside and turning down the volume on the small radio attached to her shirt. She leaned over, holding the end of her blonde ponytail, and kissed him on the cheek before she sat down.

"What happened to you?"

"That's one thing I always liked about you. You get straight to the point." He looked her over. "You look amazing. I can't believe you're here."

She looked down at her brown pants and brushed off invisible lint. "Let's just say when I heard you'd been run over by a boat, I figured there was a woman involved and I wanted to hear the story from you."

He grinned. "Hey, you know me."

"Yes, I do. And I doubt you've changed much since we were engaged. You're not a one-woman man, Joey Reed. And you never will be. It's just how you're made. But you are cute and sweet. And I forgave you long ago. I'm much happier now than I would've been going through a nasty divorce with you."

"We wouldn't have gotten divorced. I'm still not over you ditching me."

"Let's not talk about those bad memories. So, *was* it a woman who did this to you?" She grinned. He felt the urge to hold her and smell her hair, like he did years ago.

"I have no idea. I doubt it. I don't know any women with speedboats."

"She could've hired someone, you know. Us gals have been known to do those sorts of revengeful things."

He chuckled. "I was with Emma when it happened."

"I know. How is she?"

"She's good."

"Did *she* push you in front of a boat? That wouldn't surprise me, based on some of the tiffs you've told me about between the two of you. Okay, I'm just joking." She held up a hand. "I'm sorry, go ahead."

Her eyes never left his face as she asked questions and he explained. "There's no suspects."

"And you have no idea at all who might have been driving that boat?"

He shook his head. He certainly wasn't going to mention Fantasy. "I just think it was a freak accident. Emma swears the boat went right for me. And it was sitting off in a cove, in a no-wake zone. Whatever the reason, the person took off."

"I'd believe her. She's a good sleuth. You know that.

She cleaned up quite a mess in Chillicothe with the Mycons a few years back, even though she really shouldn't have been involved."

"Yeah. Thanks for helping her with that and not throwing her in jail for getting in the way."

Leila shrugged. "I'll be glad to do anything to help you find out who did this to you, too. I'm sure the force is on it. But know the offer stands."

"Thanks. I'll remember that. How're things with you? Still married, I see." He eyed her large diamond and thick wedding band.

"Yes, we're very happy. Kent got a promotion, and we may be moving to Maine." She beamed.

"Maine? It's too cold up there for you. You'll hate it," Joey said, teasingly.

"Oh, we'll adjust. His daughter's up there with the new grandbaby."

Joey looked out the window. "You know, you were the woman who broke my heart."

She chuckled and waved the comment away. "Oh, there you go again."

"No. I'm serious. I never bought a ring or proposed to another woman before or after you. You were the love of my life, Leila."

"That's all very flattering, but I don't feel a bit of remorse for ditching you. I knew you'd never settle down. And that's not what I wanted."

"I always admired you for knowing exactly what you wanted," he said.

"Too bad it wasn't the same thing," she said. Silence fell in the room before they resumed talking. Nurses came and went, checking on Joey. When the silence stretched, she stood, patted his hand, and kissed him on top of the head. "I need to go. It was good to see you."

"It's always good to see you, Leila."

She smiled, stuck her hands in her back pants pockets and rocked back on the heels of her black boots. "Get well, Joey Reed."

"I will," he said as he watched Sheriff Leila Day walk out of his life—again.

***

Merek pulled into the visitor entrance of the underground parking garage at the Tibet. He hit the button, took a parking ticket, placed it in his pocket, and rode his Harley into the garage. He parked, got off the bike, and rode the elevator up to Fantasy's floor. He walked down the hallway, aware that cameras were likely watching him every step of the way.

He stood in front of Fantasy's door and rang the buzzer. He glanced around the hallway. She'd obviously done pretty well for herself as a pole dancer at the *Messenger Club* and waiting tables at Brown's. Merek wasn't surprised. He thought of the hundred-dollar bills he'd slipped into her G-string.

She opened the door. "Merek? What are you doing here?"

"May I come in?" he asked.

She stood in the doorway, then gestured him inside. She walked ahead of him and asked if he'd like something to drink. He shook his head. "*Nie.*" He focused on her shapely tanned legs.

"Sit down," she gestured. The furniture in the living area looked modern and expensive.

Merek took a seat on the couch. "*Ładne.* Nice place."

"Thank you," she said, as she perched on the end of a chair, her hands clasped in her lap. She wore a short brown skirt and a shirt imprinted with a small Brown's Steakhouse logo. Her makeup was perfect, and her long blonde hair was pulled up into a bun. He thought about how many times he'd kissed those red lips and run his fingers through that hair.

"I hope you have been well," he said.

"Cut the chit-chat, Merek. What do you want?"

He looked around the room. "You have talked with Emma."

"Your boss. Yes. She told me about Joey and then started asking me all kinds of questions. She had no right. It was like she was accusing me of something. I don't know anything about it. Why would I? I couldn't believe it. I didn't know about it until she crashed in here and told me."

"We know you and Joey were together—dating several months ago, until he broke up with you."

She glared at him, nostrils flaring. "Just like you did. You men. You're all alike. You lead women on and then when we want to settle down and get serious, you tell us to leave you alone."

Merek took a deep breath, turned his head away, then turned back toward her. "I am here as Joey's friend, too. Like Emma. We need to find out more about his accident. To find who was in the boat. That is all."

"Why are you here? Why aren't the police here? Joey's a cop. I don't understand why his friends are asking these questions and not the cops."

"They will be here."

Fantasy jumped up from the chair and turned her back to Merek. "Why will they ask me questions? I don't own a boat. I was at work."

"You used to date Joey. And you were not at work."

She turned with her fists at her side. "I don't know what you and your boss are up to, but I want you to leave and I want both of you to leave me alone. I have to go to work now."

"Fantasy." He stood and strolled over to her. He rested a hand on her shoulder and pulled her chin up to face him. Tears welled in her eyes. "Fantasy. I am sorry for all your heartache men have brought you. You are a beautiful woman. You will find the right man. But if you know anything that might help Joey, you need to speak up about it. He did not deserve this."

She looked into his hazel eyes. Memories flowed through her mind. She thought he would ask her to marry him. But he dumped her and went to Poland. Still, she wanted him to kiss her. She closed her eyes and tilted her head back.

He pulled away and walked into the kitchen toward the refrigerator. There was no calendar, just a blank square on the door surrounded by various magnets. He glanced around, walked over to the silver trash can, opened the lid, and peered in. Empty.

Fantasy watched him before she stomped into the kitchen. She stood in front of him, pointing her finger toward his face. "Get out of here right now, Merek Polanski. And don't you or your boss ever come near me again or I will call the police and have you arrested. I have connections in high places now. You have no idea."

He held her gaze for a long moment before he clasped her finger and smiled. He walked past her out the door and made his way to his bike and rode away.

A few minutes later, he leaned against his Harley,

which was tucked in closely behind a car, about a half a block from the Tibet. He chewed on a toothpick and raised a small pair of binoculars to his eyes. He could see the front window of Fantasy's apartment and the entrance and exit to the parking garage just above the roof line of the parked car.

As he lowered the binoculars, a silver Mercedes drove past him and pulled into the tenant entrance of the parking garage, waiting for the gate to rise. Merek looked through the binoculars at the driver—a gray-haired man with a trimmed goatee. The driver looked oddly familiar, but Merek couldn't place him. He took a pen and notebook from his jacket pocket and jotted down the license-plate down on a notepad— "Esquire." He shook his head. *Another vanity plate*, he thought. He checked his watch and wrote down the time. The blinds on Fantasy's front window closed.

Two hours later, Fantasy had not left the building. Interesting, since she had to be at work. He slid his cell from his jacket pocket and punched in a number he'd remembered but deleted from his phone long ago. She picked up on the fourth ring.

"I told you to leave me alone," Fantasy yelled into the phone.

He smiled. "You still have my number in your phone after all these years," he said.

"Shut up!" The call went dead.

Merek continued to watch the entrance and exit to the complex. He was bored. He took out his cell and hit the contact on his phone for "New York Natalie."

"Merek. I was just about to call you."

"I hope for a good reason, Miss New York Natalie."

"I have what I consider good news and I hope you

will, too."

"And what is your good news?"

"I am coming to Clintonville. I am singing at a restaurant near there on Saturday night."

Merek's heart stopped. He stood straight.

"Merek? You there?"

"Yes. What a wonderful ... coincidence," he answered.

"I have to be honest. It's not a coincidence. I hope you don't mind, but I arranged it. I looked it all up on the internet and contacted the owner and sent him a video of me singing. I told him I would be in the area and asked him if I could sing there to raise money for a charity of his choice. I thought if you would like to come, it would be a win-win for everyone. If not, it will still be a win-win. I'd like to see you again, Merek Polanski. I guess I just needed an excuse. I hope I'm not being too forward."

"*Nie.* You are not being too forward. I am so happy. I will be there. You can count on it."

"That's great. And bring your friends. I was nervous when I booked it. Now I'm glad I did. Pretty scheming on my part, don't you think?"

"I like a scheming woman," he said. "Give me all the details."

As she told him about it, a shining blue metallic Mercedes GT Coupe stopped at the exit of the Tibet parking garage. He raised the binoculars. Fantasy was at the wheel.

"New York Natalie, I am glad we will see each other. But I must go now. I will call you back. I gotta scram," he said and ended the call.

The silver Mercedes with the Esquire license plate

pulled out behind her. Merek put on his gloves and helmet, waited a few seconds before firing up the Harley, and followed the silver Mercedes downtown, where it parked in a private underground lot in the Morocco Building. He sat for several minutes, surveying the area.

He rode back by Brown's Steakhouse and pulled over down the street on the other side. Fantasy's blue coupe sat in the lot. As he started to pull away, he glanced toward the entrance. The silver Mercedes he'd followed downtown pulled up at the valet and the same man and a woman walked into Brown's. He pulled out his cell and called Emma before he headed toward Calvin Nelson's.

***

"Call, please," Fantasy said as she placed the ticket in a short glass at the end of the bar. She stood scanning the dining room as the bartender made her drinks. Ian, a waiter, sauntered up to the bar and stood beside her. "Call, please," he said. He slipped his ticket in a glass and turned to Fantasy.

"Hey, Fan. How's it going? I covered your shift since you were late," he said.

"Thank you."

"It's cool. You okay?"

"Yes, I'm fine," she said, annoyed.

"Okay, okay. Just wondered since you called in that you'd be late."

"I had some unexpected business to attend to."

"It wasn't a problem. Hey, while I'm thinking about it, are you still at the Tibet?" he asked.

"Yeah. Why?"

"Just wondered. My lease is up at the end of the

month, and I looked at that place online. Man, it is pricey. Don't take this the wrong way, but how do you swing that and that fancy car you drive on this salary? You have a roommate or something?"

"Or something," she snapped.

"Okay. Whatever." Ian held up both hands in defense. They took their drink trays and went separate directions.

Minutes later, Fantasy stood at the bar again.

"Do you have a bee in your thong or what?" the bartender asked her.

"What do you mean?" she asked.

"I mean, you nearly ripped Ian's head off when he was talking to you."

"It's none of his business," she said.

"Hey, his lease is up and he's just looking for a place to live. You didn't have to be so nasty. What's up with you lately?"

"Nothing." She paused. "Yeah, I'm sorry. I have been a little short tempered."

"No need to apologize to me. Go apologize to Ian," he said.

"You're right. I will," she said, looking at the floor.

"I know it's none of my business, either. But how *do* you afford the Tibet?"

"I got an inheritance," she said.

"Oh. That's cool. I mean, I think, since someone probably died."

"Yeah. My parents left me a ton of money."

"Really? Good for you. Wait. I thought you were going to stay with your sick mom on the weekends."

"Yeah. I mean, my dad. My dad left me a bunch of money."

"So why are you bustin' your tail here?"

"I may not be for long." She had been thinking of telling Brexton she was going to quit working. She really didn't need to with all the money he gave her.

"Oh, I use that money to take care of my mom."

"He didn't leave her any?"

"They were divorced. It's complicated. You know how it is," Fantasy said, wanting the conversation to end.

"Oh, don't I? Life is complicated."

"You got that right," she said as she watched Brexton and his wife, Sheila, being seated at his regular table. "You have no idea how complicated life can be," she whispered to herself, grabbing two menus and walking toward Mr. and Mrs. Birch.

***

Emma was on the floor with her back against the loveseat. She'd hooked her laptop up to her TV and was watching Bobby's drone video for the seventh time. Chester had emailed it to her. Millie's head was in Emma's lap and the dog was snoring softly. Emma hit the rewind button again.

The video was sporadic, and it was like being on a bad amusement park ride—the lake, then tops of houses and trees, giant drops, and quick rises. Something caught her eye on a high shot. She hit the pause button once more.

"Look at that, baby girl," Emma said, zooming in on the picture with the remote. Millie didn't open her eyes but thumped her tail on the floor. "That looks like another drone. It sure does. And there's another boat below it. Way down there. You see that?"

Millie thumped her tail harder, woke up, yawned, stretched, rolled onto her side, and jammed her head into Emma's side. "Okay, okay." Emma laughed and scratched Millie's belly. Millie rolled onto her back so Emma could get a better angle.

Her cell rang. She answered, and Merek explained what he had discovered.

"You think this guy's seeing Fantasy?"

"I do not know for certain, Miss H., but everything is timing."

"I agree, timing is everything. Good work, Merek. I'll call Joey."

"I gotta scram." The call ended.

She tapped Joey's number.

"Hey, Emma."

"How are you feeling?" she asked.

"How do you think I'm feeling?"

She frowned.

"Dating any of the nurses yet?"

Joey laughed, then coughed. "Hey, don't make me laugh, okay? It hurts. Not yet, but there's a couple who may need to give me home care later on. Anyway, what are you doing?" he asked.

"I'm watching a drone video that a grandpa emailed me."

"What did you say?" Joey asked.

"While I was kayaking at the scene today, I met a guy and his grandson. They had a drone with a camera on it, and they happened to be using it on Saturday morning. I explained the situation, and grandpa Chester was more than happy to email me the video."

"Can you see the driver of the boat?" he asked.

"No. But I'm pretty sure I see another drone and

another boat, further upstream from where we were. People on that boat may have seen or heard something or have something on their drone video. I can't make out that boat at all. It's just a dot."

"Too bad. Could be witnesses. Drones. They're getting pretty popular, from what I've been reading."

"I know. I've read that, too. Amazon's even testing them to deliver packages. Pretty wild. And this is proof— two drones within minutes. Should I send this to Miles and see what he can do with it?"

"Sounds good. I'll let him know. Anything else?"

"Yeah, Merek went to chat with Fantasy. He said it was apparent there'd likely been a calendar on her refrigerator door, but it was gone. Just a blank square, surrounded by magnets. Then she kicked him out. He stuck around, waiting for her to leave since she said she had to go to work. He was going to go to Brown's and maybe talk to her there. She was dressed to go to work when he talked to her at her place."

"Yeah, and?" Joey asked.

"She didn't leave. Right away, anyway. While he was waiting, a gray-haired man with a goatee pulled into the Tibet. Merek said the guy looked a little familiar, but he didn't know why. He also thought it odd that someone who looked like that, with the license plate "Esquire," would be going home rather than going to an office. Right before the car passed him, Fantasy closed her front shades. He said he had a funny feeling about it all, so he stuck around. Two hours later, this man pulls out right behind our girl, who is driving a hundred thousand-dollar Mercedes coupe. She must make really good money as a waitress to be living this lifestyle. Merek tailed the guy to the Morocco building downtown and then went back to

Brown's."

"Hmmm… Did you have Miles run the plates?"

"Yep."

"And?"

"And the guy that owns the car is Brexton Birch. And his law firm is in the Morocco. Merek said he finally recognized him from all those hokey TV commercials for Birch and Taylor."

"Brexton Birch." Joey chuckled. "Well, well. I know who he is. I did a little work for him and his partner, Leonard, a few years back on some high-end divorce case. They're the biggest alimony shop in town. Merek never actually saw him with Fantasy, did he?"

"No, but I'm not finished. Later, Merek went to Brown's and hung around outside. He said Fantasy's fancy little car was in the lot and that Brexton walked in with a woman he figures is his wife, Sheila—*the* Mrs. Birch. That's sort of weird if he's boinking Fantasy, don't you think? Why would you take your wife to a place your mistress works? But I don't think it's a coincidence, do you?"

"Could be. But, yeah, a weird one. Lots of people go to Brown's for lunch. And Brexton Birch could have a place at the Tibet."

"He does. Merek checked."

"Could be he and Fantasy just know each other from living in the same building and they just happened to go to lunch at Brown's. Maybe Fantasy invited them."

"Come on, Joey. Out of all the people Merek sees today, two of them live at the same place, leave their condos at the same time, and show up at the same place for lunch. And Sheila wasn't with Brexton at the Tibet. It's just too weird."

"Yeah, okay. I hear you. Merek does good work."

"I know. He's checking to see if Brexie owns a boat."

"Keep on this, okay? We don't have any proof of anything except Birch and Fantasy both have apartments at the Tibet."

"And drive an expensive Mercedes. But I know that doesn't mean they ran over you in a boat," she said.

"Hey, not to change the subject, but you'll never guess who was here today," Joey said.

"Another one of your women?"

"As a matter of fact, yes. *The woman*."

"And who would *the woman* be?"

"Come on, Emma. You know I only bought a ring once in my life."

Emma paused, thinking. "Day?"

"Yep. She came to see me. You can't tell me she still doesn't still have feelings for me. Anyway, it was good to see her. She still looks great. Said she'd do anything she could to help. She also said they were moving to Maine. Can you believe that? Who would move to Maine? Nothing up there but snow and moose. And his grandkid."

"Wow. She's got a grandkid?"

"Well, it's his. She married some old fart."

"Joey, we're old farts, too. We'll both be fifty in a few years. Think about it."

"Hey, sorry. I didn't mean to ... You know. Stratton and all. He's not an old fart."

"No problem."

"He coming home soon?"

"I've no idea. I haven't talked to him in a while," she said.

"Oh. Okay," he said.

"Look, everything's fine. We just need to find who

ran over you. That's all I'm thinking about right now," she said.

"Fine. Look, just tell Merek thanks. I'm sure it was probably uncomfortable for him going to see Fantasy."

"He didn't sound like it bothered him at all. He sounded sort of amused."

"Good. Hey, here comes my doctor who can't keep her hands off me. Call me when you find out more."

"Sure will. I'll stop in soon. Bye." She laid the cell back on the side table and looked down at Millie. "That was Uncle Joey. He's busy hitting on his doctor."

Millie stood and gave herself a good shake and yawned.

"Yeah, I know. Some things never change, do they, baby girl?"

***

Merek got off his bike and tossed his gloves into his helmet. He ran a hand over his head, tucked the helmet under his left arm, and took in the neighborhood. It was a typical, cookie-cutter McMansion suburb with huge houses that all looked the same. Merek admired the meticulous landscaping but was glad he didn't have to deal with yard work in his high-rise condo.

He took the slip of paper he'd written Calvin's address on and checked it again before he rang the doorbell. He heard movement inside, and the door opened. Calvin wore a Hawaiian shirt, red shorts, and flip-flops. His white hair plugs were gelled back, and the gold chain around his neck gleamed in the sun. He reeked of cologne. He frowned up at Merek, who was nearly two feet taller than Calvin.

"What are you doing here? Where's Emma?"

"Emma is busy. She sent me to have lunch with you and review the presentation."

Calvin blinked. "That's ridiculous. I expect her to be here. Where is she? I told *her* to be here, and I expect *her* to be here." He pointed toward the ground.

"She is busy. So, I am here. May I come in?" Merek smiled and pointed at himself.

Calvin stood for a few seconds before he turned toward the inside of the house and then back to Merek. He shook his head, then shrugged. "I guess so. Okay, come on in." He reluctantly motioned Merek inside.

"Good. I am starving," Merek said.

"Well, goodie for you," Calvin said as he shut the door behind them. "I don't suppose you could take off those heavy boots before you tromp through my foyer, could you?"

Merek chuckled. "The stink of my feet will be worse than the boots on your floor, Mr. Calvin."

Calvin looked up at him and wrinkled his face. He gestured toward Merek. "How can you stand to wear all that leather in this heat?"

Merek shrugged. "I get used to it. But I will take off my jacket."

Calvin said nothing for several seconds. "Yeah, okay. Take off the coat. Give it to me, and I'll put it in the closet."

"That is not necessary. I will keep it."

Calvin gave him a disgusted look. "Fine, fine. Do whatever you want. Let's go in my office and I'll show you what I need changed."

"The food smells delicious," Merek said as he shrugged off his jacket, moving his helmet from arm to arm, following Calvin. Calvin stopped and turned toward him. He looked Merek up and down, clearly uncomfortable.

"Yeah. Well, all right. We may as well eat it since you're hungry and it's already made. I'm hungry, too."

"That is good," Merek said, smiling at Calvin's back. "Thank you."

They walked into the kitchen. Merek heard someone singing "I'm in the Mood for Love," before Calvin flipped off the music playing on a Bose sitting on the back countertop. "Sit at the counter."

Merek sat and laid his jacket and helmet on the chair next to him. Calvin busied himself with take-out containers, his back to Merek. "You want a beer? I don't have any of that Polish crap you probably drink. I only have good stuff."

"*Żywiec*. That is my favorite beer. It is good beer."

"Yeah, yeah. Whatever."

"I will not be drinking," Merek said.

"Good for you. I'm gonna have one and probably several more—now," Calvin said.

"I would like water, please," Merek said. He turned around, examining the surroundings. The table was set with red dishes and cloth napkins. A huge vase of roses sat to the side of the place settings. A bottle was chilling in a silver bucket, the condensation beading on the sides. Merek grinned to himself.

"Miss Emma was very sorry she could not make it," Merek said.

Calvin got a glass from the cupboard and pushed it against the refrigerator door, filling it with crushed ice and water. He set the glass in front of Merek. "I'll bet. Let's cut the bullshit, Merek. Man to man. I want her. I want her bad. And I'll do what it takes to get her. And I will get her, eventually. She just has to get to know me better, is all. I mean, look at me. What's not to love? I got women all over me, all the time. But I want Emma Haines. And I'll get her. Hell, I want to marry her." Calvin gave Merek a little salute with his beer bottle before he took a swig.

"But what about Mr. Stratton?"

Calvin grinned. "I think there's trouble in paradise. Why isn't she with *Mr. Stratton* if they're so in love? Maybe she dumped him. You know anything about that?"

Merek shook his head. "I cannot say. That is Emma's business." He took a long drink of water. The tattoos on his neck moved with every swallow. Calvin watched, mesmerized.

"I just gotta ask you something. You got those tattoos all over your body?" He glanced at Merek's neck and arms below the T-shirt sleeves, and the tops of his hands. His brothers had given him the shirt when he left Poland. It read, *Urodzony do Jazdy*—Born to Ride.

Merek shrugged. "I have many. I like them."

"I couldn't tell. You got a lot of money in those things, I'll bet. A lot of Matrix's money."

Merek looked around the kitchen and drank the water.

"So, you got them *everywhere*?" Calvin smiled like an evil child and took a sip of his beer.

Merek didn't smile back. "What is for lunch?"

"That's okay. We're not buddies. Hell, I don't even like you. You don't have to tell me. But I'll bet you do have them *everywhere*. You look like the type."

Merek emptied his water. "May I have more water,

please?"

"Yeah, sure. Sure."

Calvin placed another glass of water in front of Merek and turned back to the kitchen counter. He spooned Chinese food from take-out boxes onto plates. He placed a plate of food and a fork in front of Merek. Calvin leaned against the sink with his plate in front of his chest, facing Merek. He shoveled food into his mouth and chewed.

"May we sit at the table?" Merek asked.

"No. You're good right there. Let's eat and get to that presentation. I got a lot to do today," Calvin mumbled through chewing.

"May I have a napkin?" Merek asked.

Calvin looked annoyed, put down his food, rummaged through a drawer, and tossed a bag of paper napkins on the counter. They ate in silence. After a long moment, Calvin said, "I have to ask—you and Emma ever … you know …?" He smiled and wobbled his hand back and forth.

Merek put his fork on his plate. "Emma is my business partner. We have never been lovers. As you Americans say, I do not fill my baskets with every egg."

Calvin snorted. "You mean you don't put all your eggs in one basket or shit in your nest. Okay. I'll give you that."

They both continued to eat.

"Yeah. Emma's beautiful. She's a real pistol. I love it when she gets feisty. I can't imagine her in the sack, can you?" Calvin smiled at Merek and waved his butt like a duck coming out of the water.

Merek placed his fork on his plate again and stood. Calvin backed up as they glared at each other.

Merek walked around the kitchen island and towered over Calvin. "You do not talk about Miss Emma in this manner to me or anyone else. And you leave her alone or I will break your face, Mr. Calvin Nelson. Do you—the smart American with only the good stuff—understand this? You send me the changes for the presentation, and I will make them and send them back."

Merek picked up his jacket and helmet, walked down the hallway, and slammed the door behind him.

***

Brexton Birch held his fifth drink between his left thumb and middle finger and gazed into it. He moved the glass slowly. The honey-colored whiskey flowed around the ice. He liked the weight of the crystal glass and the way the ice tinkled against its sides.

His thoughts wouldn't let go—how would he rid himself from the best sex he'd ever known? Sadly, it was attached to the most beautiful and crazy woman he'd ever met.

Leonard Taylor, childhood friend and firm partner since they graduated from law school, slid into the seat on the other side of the booth, holding a bottle of Heineken.

"Man, what a day," Leonard said. "This divorce case is not worth all the energy I'm putting into it, no matter how much I'll get out of it. My daughter's coming into town tomorrow. I haven't seen her for six months. She's been in China studying. Proud of her, you know? I'm real proud of her. Anyway, the only time I could give her was maybe a quick lunch. Pathetic, isn't it? You raise a kid and then neither of you have time to even talk to each other.

And I wasn't home that much when she was growing up. Work, work, work. It's crazy. You don't have kids, so you don't understand."

He took a swig of beer and set the bottle on the table. He examined the label. "I need to pick up a six-pack of this. Remember when we had our first Heiny together, Brex? Oh, man. I do. Those were the days, you know?" He picked up the bottle and drank again. "Never liked any other kind of beer. Crazy, but it's true. And I should know. I've tried them all. They're all good, but not like a Heiny."

He glanced at Brexton, who continued to watch the liquid in his glass as he moved it around slowly.

"Brex? Man? You okay? You look like shit. How many of those have you had?"

Brexton didn't answer. He continued to move the glass and stare at it. After a few seconds, he knocked back the rest of the drink and put the empty glass on the table.

"This is the drink I had after the last one … and before the next one," he slurred.

"And how many does that make?"

"It will make it the …" he closed his eyes and shook his head. "I dunno."

"You got the Uber app on your phone, right?"

Brexton nodded.

"Use it. Probably wouldn't look too good for one of the attorneys in the biggest law firm in town getting a DUI."

Brexton shrugged. "I can't leave my Mercedes here. Sheeeeelaaah would accuse me of selling it or something." His glass was empty. "Can you flag down David?"

"Yes, I can. But you're done. You've had enough. What's wrong with you? You need money again?"

Brexton shook his head.

"Good. You been gambling again?"

Brexton made a horse sound with his lips. "I wish it were that simple. This is much worse than my little gambling habit."

"Must be bad then. That million and a half bet on the ponies was a little over the top." Leonard took another drink of beer and waved the waiter over to the table. "Hi, David. How's it going?"

The waiter smiled as he smoothed his tie. "Good, good. You gentlemen doing okay?"

"Yeah. We're good. I'll have another one of these and my friend here will have coffee—straight up, black and strong."

"Sure thing, Mr. Taylor. Be right back with those."

Leonard glanced around the room. "Well, at least there's not many people in here tonight. Still, you need to watch, it, Brex. People in this town know us. I'll probably have to carry you home. Forget Uber. What's going on?"

"Sheila. I can't stand her. I despise her."

"What else is new? What'd she do now? Scratch the pink Porsche you bought her last month? God, who in their right mind would do that to such a gorgeous car? Pink, I mean … Damn." He sipped his beer, watching Brexton. "What gives?"

"Women."

"What about them?"

"A woman."

"Oh, shit," Leonard said, shaking his head.

"Yes."

"Hooker?"

"I wish."

"What? You think you're in love or something stupid?"

"No. Lust. Pure lust. I can't describe it. She's gorgeous and wonderful."

Leonard rolled his eyes. "It'll wear off. Give it time."

Brexton shook his head. "It won't. But I have to end it. Now. This woman is crazy. I tried to reason with her earlier today, but she's out of control. A possessive maniac. She texts me constantly. I saw her loitering in the lobby one day." He rubbed his face.

"Ain't that the way it goes? Why'd you go for a crazy one? You should've stuck to the high-end call girls. They know the rules."

"Dunno. She seemed sane enough," Brexton mumbled.

"How long you been seeing this broad?"

Brexton looked at the ceiling. "Far too long, that's for sure."

"How long?"

"About three months. I set her up in a condo at the Tibet in her name, down the hall from mine. It's perfect, really. Sheila knows I stay in my condo when I work late. She doesn't want me driving home after a hard day, making millions of dollars so she can spend it. Frankly, I'd be worth more to her dead. It's too bad she's still in love with me. Anyway, Fantasy—"

"Fantasy?" Leonard laughed loudly. "I thought you said she wasn't a hooker."

"She's not. She's a waitress at Brown's. That's where I met her. She used to be a dancer at the Messenger."

Leonard shook his head. "You're really moving up in the world, Brex."

Brexton gave him a look. "I wanted her the instant I

saw her. And today, Sheila came into my office and insisted I take her to Brown's for lunch and Fantasy was our waitress. I'd just left the condo after being with her all morning. But she acted like it didn't bother her at all. She talked to Sheila like they were old friends—Fantasy flitting around the table, complimenting Sheila on her dress and shoes. I wanted to scream." His words ran together.

"I can't believe you took that big of a gamble. This Fantasy could've blown it all for you right there with Sheila."

Brexton shook his head. "Nothing doing. I dump four grand into her checking account for rent every month to pay for that condo and another three grand for her to play with as long as she keeps her mouth shut. I bought her a fun little car. No matter what. That was the deal. She's not dumb enough to blow that."

"Do you think Sheila suspects anything about you and this Fantasy chick?"

"No, I'm certain she doesn't. She's too busy spending my money. When she's not spending my money, she's bitching at me about not making enough money. And I'm safe at the Tibet. She hates the place and told me to never expect her to come to those 'cheap apartments.' The condos cost more, a *lot* more, than our house on the lake, and I'm paying for all of them. I can't take her anymore, Len. I just can't," Brexton said, his chin nearly on his chest.

"What are you saying? That you're finally going to ask for a divorce? No way, man. You crazy? She'll ruin you. She'll ruin the firm. She'll ruin me. No way. You can't do that. You going to leave her for this new Fantasy nut of yours? Are you crazy?"

Brexton shook his head. "No. You're right. I can't.

I'll be married to that money-hungry bitch forever. I have to get rid of Fantasy. But it gets worse," he said so low that Leonard barely heard him.

"How much worse can this get?" Leonard, said. He glanced around then leaned across the table toward Brexton and lowered his voice.

"What are you talking about, Brex?"

"A video," Brexton whispered.

"What?" Leonard threw himself back in his seat and smacked his forehead. "You did it again? You took a video of you guys making out and now she's blackmailing you? Again? I thought you said *she* was the crazy one."

"No. Nothing like that."

"I still can't believe you did that with that one chick. Talk about dumb. You've got some sick thing going on. I'm surprised you're still not paying that one off."

Brexton interrupted. "That's old news, Lenny. This is much worse. If she goes to the police about this video, I'm more than ruined."

"If it's not the two of you, then what's on *this* video?"

Brexton paused. "Fantasy and I were on my boat and ..." he trailed off as David came to the table and set another bottle of beer in front of Leonard and steaming black coffee in front of Brexton.

"I know you don't like your beer in a glass, Mr. Taylor," the waiter said.

"That's why I come here, David. Because you remember these things." Leonard downed the last of his beer and handed him the empty bottle.

David beamed. "Will there be anything else, gentlemen?"

"No, thanks. We'll just pay up. You can put his tab on my card," Leonard said, nodding toward Brexton. He pulled a credit card from his wallet and handed it to David.

"Will do, Mr. Taylor," David said and left the table.

"Thank you," Brexton mumbled to Leonard.

"Yeah, whatever. You need to stop drinking so much. Anyway, you were saying." He motioned for Brexton to keep talking.

"I met her early in the morning, before anyone would be around. We were just floating on the boat, eating a little breakfast, having a wonderful time. She looked so good in that bikini."

"Yeah, yeah, whatever. Get back to the video."

"I was flying my drone with the camera around the lake—just for fun, you know?" His hand was shaking as he brought the coffee cup to his lips and took a sip. He set the cup in the saucer with a clank. "It accidentally captured a video of a boating accident."

"A drone. You and your toys. Wait. Boating accident. The one in Sunday's paper? Lieutenant Reed?"

Brexton nodded without looking up.

"Well, you've got to turn it in. Reed's a good guy. He's helped us with a few cases. The cops are asking for information."

"I can't do that. I was supposed to be in the office Saturday morning, and there was a time stamp on that video. The video caught Fantasy and me talking and laughing on it, too. I didn't know what was on it until we both watched it after I got the drone back on the boat. It's not like I can take it to someone to *edit*. He took another sip of coffee and made a bitter face.

"It was apparent in the video that the boat was sitting on the other side of the reservoir, and when Reed paddled out into the lake, the boater went right for him, ran over him, and sped away. The drone was too high to make out anything else, but that much was clear."

"Wait." He ran his fingers through his hair and sat back in the booth. "You told Sheila you were at the office, but ... you were with ... this Fantasy chick and you are now both technically witnesses and you have evidence."

"Exactly. But I can't get involved. And to make matters even worse, Fantasy used to date Reed. What are the odds? She insists that I turn in the video. But I erased it. But she doesn't know that. Still, *we can't get involved—neither of us*," he said through gritted teeth.

"Can you pick 'em or what? You're keeping a former pole dancer that used to date a top cop in Clintonville. You took her out on your boat and now you two are witnesses to his accident. Amazing. Simply amazing. You can't make this shit up," Leonard said. He shook his head before he took a large drink of beer.

Brexton sipped his coffee. He placed the cup in the saucer with a clatter and ran his fingers through his hair and rubbed his face. He let out a long sigh.

Leonard drank his beer as he eyed Brexton. After nearly a minute, he asked, "What are you going to do, Brex?"

Wednesday

"WHY ARE YOU wearing that getup?" Emma asked Merek as she slid into the booth at the Wildflower Café at eight in the morning. He wore jeans, a long-sleeve blue, shirt, and a pair of blue Vans sneakers—not his normal leather attire.

"I am going to go to the Tibet again. More surveillance. Less conspicuous. I look like a stuffy businessman."

"Ahhhh. Good thinking. Incognito," Emma smiled as she looked over the menu.

Merek handed her several sheets of stapled papers. "Here is the list of all the boat owners in the county. A separate sheet for people living with a dock and a direct way to the water is the top page."

"This is great, Merek. Thanks for having Miles send you this," Emma said. The waitress came by and filled her cup with coffee. Emma looked up. "Thanks, Autumn. Appreciate it." Emma and Merek placed their orders.

"Sure thing. You want more coffee, Merek?" Autumn asked.

"Tak, proszę."

She poured. "I've learned that much over the years. But don't expect me to tell you in Polish, 'you're welcome' even though you've taught me how to say it. You look really different, all dressed up, Merek. I hardly recognized you. You look really nice." She smiled and blushed. "Your orders will be right out."

"That Mr. Birch—he owns a boat and lives along that lake," Merek said.

"What? That's huge. I'll go check it out. Joey may be right. Maybe Fantasy did have Birch run over him." She paused, thinking. "But I still can't buy it. A man like Birch just wouldn't risk everything for a chick like her. And why would she want to blow such a good setup?" She paused, then continued.

"Do you think Fantasy really could have talked Brexton Birch into running over Joey? Why didn't she just have him shoot him or something easier? Why this? It's just too risky. There could've been witnesses out there. And Birch is a top dog in town. I just can't buy it. Could Birch be *that* jealous of Joey?"

Merek shrugged. "She is a beautiful woman."

"She ain't *that* beautiful."

Merek drank his coffee.

"Would you have tried to kill someone for her if she wanted you to?"

He shook his head and laughed. "*"Nie wydaje mi się"*. But we do not know the story with them."

"True. I'm going to go check out the Birch place, then see Joey after we eat. I want to tell him about the boat in person. Why don't you visit the marinas and see if anyone's seen a boat that may have been in for repairs or something."

"And I will go back to talk to Fantasy this morning.

I will find out more," he said.

"I hope so."

"Here you go," Autumn said, setting their plates in front of them. "Veggie omelet for you, Emma, and the burrito and the steak and eggs for you. Be careful, Merek, it's really hot."

"*Dziękuję*," he replied.

"I'll be right back with your hot sauce," she said and left.

"How do you eat like that and look as good as you do? You remind me of Stratton," she said.

He smiled. "I spend much time in the gym."

"I'll bet. Explains those arms of yours. They look like tattooed logs."

He took a huge bite of his burrito.

"I think she likes you," Emma said, nodding toward Autumn.

Merek chewed.

"Too bad she's not blonde. Speaking of which, what blonde babe are you dating now?" Emma asked.

He gave her a look, chewed, swallowed. "I am not dating anyone. But I am in love."

She put her fork down and propped her chin in her hand. "Please don't tell me Ludnella's back."

He shook his head. "*Nie.*" He paused. "Do you remember Natalie? I met her at the old store in Kentucky."

"What? Really? You're in love with *her*? Someone you met for what, twenty minutes and talked to on the phone once? I thought you said she was married and lived in New York."

He thanked Autumn as she put the bottle of hot sauce on the table beside him.

"Anything else, folks?' Autumn asked.

"No, we're good," Emma said. Merek agreed.

"Okay." Autumn gave Merek another long look before she turned to leave. Merek was too busy opening the bottle of Frank's Red Hot sauce to notice. He shook a large amount on his food, then looked up at Emma.

"She is now divorced." He explained everything as they ate. It always amazed Emma how well Merek spoke English, and she loved his Polish accent. He had an American friend in Poland he had worked with at a grocery store who taught him English and told him all about The Ohio State University, where he studied Polish.

"And she is coming here Saturday morning. She is singing at the Worthington Inn that night." His smile lit up the booth, if not the entire restaurant.

"What? This is amazing. How did all this happen? You are a total chick magnet."

"Miss H., I am no magnet."

"Well, yeah, you are. Anyway, this woman is a lot different from your others."

"*Wiem.* She has two children."

"Wow. That's huge, you know. And an ex-husband?"

"*Tak.*"

"And she lives in New York City. How did it happen that she's playing here on Saturday?"

He filled her in.

"Oh, boy. She wants you. Be careful. A single woman with two kids. And if she's as beautiful as you say she is … nothing against you, my Polish stud man, but look out. She's probably trolling for a kid daddy."

"That is fine. I would love to be their father."

"What? Wait a minute, Merek. You need to really think about this. This is a big step, dating this 'New York

Natalie' woman. And you don't even know her or her kids."

"I know. But I am ready. I am tired of blonde dancers. I want to settle down and have a family."

"Seems to be going around. Since when do you want to settle down?"

He shrugged.

She ate, leaned back, and sipped her coffee. "How was your lunch with Calvin?"

Merek made a face, "*Straszne,*" he said. "The man, he is a *świnia.*"

"That good, huh? Thanks for going, by the way." She patted his arm.

"I do not like Mr. Calvin."

"I don't, either. But Mr. Matrix adores him. Even though he's a jerk, he knows the claims business. I'll give him that. And Matrix pays us. But he is pretty nasty, isn't he?"

"*Zgadzam się.* You have no idea, Miss H."

***

Joey counted the cars going up the ramp in the parking garage. He wondered how long it would be until he would be driving again. Or walking. Or jogging. His doctor—and hopefully new love in his life—told him he was coming along nicely and should heal with no problems. But he couldn't help wondering if he might have a permanent limp like Charles's former beau, Ron. And he wondered how the injuries might impact his job. *How could Fantasy have done this?* He couldn't get the thought out of his mind.

Emma tapped on the door. He didn't turn his head to see who it was. Today, he didn't care.

"Hey, there. Okay if I come in? I have news."

He slowly turned his head toward her.

"You okay?" she asked.

"I guess. I'm just really tired of being in here. I'm just feeling down."

"I'm sorry," she said. "But this is pretty important."

He motioned here in. "Okay. What do you got?" He hit a button, and the bed groaned as it lifted him into a sitting position.

"Merek asked Miles to get him the names of boat owners in Franklin County and separate those who live around the reservoir. You can guess who has one." She handed him the stapled sheets of paper.

"Brexton Birch."

"Yep," she said.

"Doesn't really surprise me. He's probably doing okay. Lots of wealthy people have boats and live by the water. But not lots of people who have a condo in the same building with Fantasy and eats lunch where she works and has a house along the lake where I was plowed over." Joey sighed. "She got Brexton Birch to run over me with his boat for revenge."

Emma shook her head. "I don't think so, even though Birch has a white boat with a windshield. I didn't see a Bimini, but he could've taken it off. I snuck around to the back of his house and checked it out on my way over here."

"There's laws against trespassing, you know?" He grinned.

Emma rolled her eyes. "Why run over you with a boat? There are much easier ways to kill people. And why would he risk his entire life for someone like Fantasy? Do you really think she has that kind of power and was that mad at you?"

He gave her a look. "Revenge is a powerful thing."

"True. But we don't even know if they know each other yet, for sure. But Merek's over at her place right now and he's going to talk to her again," she said.

"That's good of him to do that. I appreciate you guys doing this for me. I just don't want to waste my men's time downtown. They have more important things to do." He laid the list of boatowners on the side table. "I'll look at this later. I'm not in the mood right now. But tell Merek and Miles thanks."

"We need solid proof, Joey. You know that."

"You're right. Okay, just keep working on it, please. I've been thinking a lot about it. I think it's them. She knew we were going to be out there and she told him and he did it. She can charm a snake out of its skin. Trust me on that one." He let out a deep breath and closed his eyes. "Damn, I was hoping it wasn't her. Can I pick 'em or what?" He threw his head back into the pillow.

They fell quiet.

She patted his shoulder. "I was wondering if it would be okay if I talked to your buddies at the shop, Sammy and Cook."

Joey looked perplexed. "Why?"

She shrugged. "I don't know. Maybe they mentioned that you were going kayaking to someone. I'd planned on talking to them before all this Brexton stuff came up. It wouldn't hurt."

"I don't see what good it'll do, but you can go downtown and talk to them. It's okay."

"Okay. I'll stop there when I leave here. Will they be there?"

"They should be. Let me check." He picked up his

cell from the hospital table and hit a number.

"Yeah, Cook, it's Joey. Yeah. Okay. Yeah." There was more talk about Joey's condition and small talk before he told him Emma was helping with the investigation and asked if it would it be okay if she stopped by to talk with them.

"Great. Thanks. I'll let her know. She'll be there in about half an hour. Thanks, Cook." A pause. "Yeah, I will. Take care. Okay." He ended the call.

"You heard it. They'll be there."

"Okay. You sure there's nothing you need?" she said.

"Nope. I'm fine." He smiled—not the normal Joey Reed smile. "Maybe another Big Mac?"

"You got it. But it might be tomorrow before I get back here. It'll give you something to look forward to. And I'll let you know what Merek finds out."

"Right. Okay, then. Tell the guys I said hello."

"I will."

He watched Emma leave the room. He turned toward the window. *Fantasy had the top lawyer in town run over me. This will look just great for everyone. What was Birch thinking?* He hit the bed with a fist.

A few hours later, a nurse woke him. After she left, he picked up the list of boat owners and flipped through several pages. One of the names caused him to pause.

***

Emma knocked on the door jam. Sammy and Cook sat at facing desks.

"Hey, there. I'm Emma Haines. Okay if I come in?"

They looked up from paperwork. The red-headed

man who looked like he could be considering retirement soon stood and said, "Sure, come on in. Joey talked to Cook and said you'd be stopping by." He walked around the desk and put out a hand. "I'm Sam Heath. Everyone calls me Sammy. Pleased to meet you." Emma shook his hand.

Cook, also an older officer, had thinning gray hair. He walked over and said, "I'm Wilbur Cook. Pleased to meet you." They shook hands. "Please, have a seat. Can I get you anything? Pepsi? Coffee? Water?"

Emma shook her head. "No, I'm fine, thanks."

He sat on the corner of the desk after Emma sat. Sammy walked back around his desk and sat in his chair. He leaned forward. "Joey has always spoken very highly of you over the years. He told us about you starting your own business called H.I.T. Bad deal this happened to him. How can we help?"

"I learned everything I know from Joey. Thanks for seeing me. As you know, I'm trying to find out who was driving that boat."

"That's good of you. Joey says since we're under-staffed, he wants us to work on more important cases. We all think his is pretty important, but we're not in charge. He's the boss, not us," Sammy said with a shrug. "Otherwise, we'd be on it more."

"I understand. It's no problem for me to look into it." She paused, then continued. "Joey told me he was joking around with you both about him going kayaking, and I was just wondering if you might've mentioned it to anyone."

Cook put his chin in a chubby hand. Sammy made a deep-thinking face. After a few seconds, Cook said, "I told my wife. We were talking over dinner last week about it and she said she'd like to try it someday, too. Maybe something to do when we retire in a few months. We talked about that. But nothing more."

"Could she have told someone? I know I'm reaching for straws here, but I'm just trying to cover all the bases. I'm sure you guys understand."

They both nodded. "Sure," Cook said. "I doubt it, but I can ask her."

Sammy said "I don't think I said a word about it to anyone. I never gave it any thought except when we were laughing about it here in the office. Joey's not known for being an outdoor adventurer. We all got a kick out of it."

Emma smiled. "He's bugged me to go for years, but I ignored him. I wish I would've ignored him this time."

"You can't blame yourself. It was probably a crazy accident and the person or people on the boat took off. We keep putting word out through the media. We've offered a reward for information. We've had several calls and checked them out. Nothing solid. That's all I can tell you. You understand," Cook said.

"I understand. Anything out of the ordinary happen last week? Anything at all?" Emma asked.

They both shook their heads. "No, none that I recall," Sammy said.

Emma stood. "Well, if you think of anything, I'm sure you'll let Joey know."

"Absolutely. I'm sure he appreciates you trying to help. Any leads on your end, I'm sure you'll let us know."

"First thing," she lied. She wasn't going to mention Fantasy and Brexton Birch—not yet. That was Joey's call.

"Thanks for talking with me." She stood to leave.

"Sure thing," Cook said. As he walked her to the

doorway, an older, tall, bald man walked through the hallway toward them.

Cook looked past her and said, "Hey, James. Good to see you. We went to that restaurant Saturday night. The one you told me about when you were here Thursday. You were right. It was good."

"Fine, fine. Did you have the ribeye?"

Cook shook his head. "No, but the fish special was delicious."

"That's good. I've never had a bad meal there," the man said.

They turned their attention to Emma. Cook introduced them. "James, this is Emma Haines. She's a close friend of Joey Reed. She and Joey investigated cases together when she worked in the fraud department at Matrix Insurance. Now, she owns a consulting company called H.I.T. She's trying to help find out who ran over him on Saturday. She was with him when it happened. Emma, this is James Mars, retired detective. One of the best."

"Pleased to meet you," Emma said, shaking the man's hand. He was in good shape for being in his seventies, she guessed.

"Yes. Terrible accident. So sorry to hear about it. I read about it in the paper. I'm sure these fine detectives will find the person who was driving that boat."

"Yes, I'm sure they will," she said before turning to Cook. "Thanks again."

As Emma walked down the hallway of the police station and opened the door, her cell buzzed. She pulled it from her purse, looked at the screen and rolled her eyes. She stood on the step, looked at the blue sky with white puffs of clouds, took a deep breath, and hit the accept call icon.

"What's up, Calvin?"

"Your so-called partner is what's up. Why didn't you come to my house? Why'd you send your punk?"

She walked down the steps of the Clintonville police station into the parking lot toward her truck as she continued the conversation. "Are there more changes to the presentation?"

"No. He sent them. I just want to know why you stood me up for lunch. That wasn't very nice of you, Emma."

"I had to be someplace else. I'm working a case."

"Hummffff." He paused. "Have you heard from Stratton lately?"

"Is this a business call, Calvin? Because if it's not, I'm hanging up."

"Just keep your Polish thug away from me. I don't like him."

"Merek's not a thug or a punk. What'd he ever do that upset you?"

"Nothing. I just don't like him. He's a thug."

"He is not a *thug*. Stop saying that. And if you want to deal with me, you'll deal with Merek, too, or find someone else to help train your investigators. Is that all?" she said.

A pause.

"That's it for now," he said.

"Fine." She nearly shouted and ended the call.

***

Sheila Birch stood behind a tree across the street from the Tibet. She lowered the binoculars from her eyes and took a deep breath. "How stupid does he think I am?" she said aloud.

She pulled her phone from her jeans pocket and hit Brexton's cell number. She put the binoculars up to her eyes again as she held the phone to her ear. She watched him dig the phone from his jacket pocket, check it, look up and say something to a blonde, and turn back toward the window. The woman disappeared from sight.

"Yes, dear. What is it? I'm very busy," Brexton said.

"I didn't call the office because you said you'd be at the courthouse this morning. I'm assuming, that's where you are."

"Yes. In fact, we're in the middle of a meeting. What do you want, Sheila?"

It was all she could do not to tell him to look out the window and wave at him. Or to scream, "*LIAR!*" into the phone as she watched him pace in front of the window.

"I need you to go by the bakery tonight on your way home. I ordered a cake for dinner this evening, and I won't have time to pick it up. Remember the Longs are arriving at six. I'm working at the hospital desk this afternoon, you know," Sheila said.

He lifted his head and held the bridge of his nose. "Yes. Yes, I can do that. Is that all?"

"For now," she said and ended the call, watching him through the window.

He shook his head and put the phone back in his jacket pocket before the woman came back and they stood kissing in front of the window.

Sheila lowered the binoculars.

***

Merek looked through his binoculars. He was parked in an alley with a good view of the entrance and exit of the Tibet.

He checked his watch. At a quarter after nine, the silver Mercedes with the Esquire license plate entered the tenant side of the garage, driven by Brexton Birch. Merek put his binoculars in a saddlebag and walked down the street toward the entrance. He pretended to be looking at his cellphone as he went into the parking garage. Once inside, he slid his cell into his back pocket.

A car engine stopped, and a car door shut. Heels clicked above him. Merek jogged and hid behind the elevator wall, watching as Brexton Birch pushed the button. Seconds later, he entered the elevator. Merek jogged to the elevator just as the door shut. It went to the same floor as Fantasy's. He turned and walked out of the parking garage. No one approached him or asked him any questions as he sauntered down the block, back to his bike.

He got his binoculars and scanned the building. Bingo. Fantasy's blinds were open, and she walked past her window. He focused. Moments later, Brexton Birch stood in front of the window. He pulled out his phone, said something to Fantasy, and turned toward the window and took the call. Merek watched as Birch talked and held the bridge of his nose. After he put the phone away, Fantasy walked into his arms and they kissed.

Merek lowered the binoculars, slid his cell from his pocket, and called Emma.

***

Fantasy traced circles with a long, silver fingernail on Brexton's chest as they lay in her bed. She snuggled closer to him.

"Brexton, you are the best man I've ever known."

He said nothing.

"I love you so much."

Silence.

"Fantasy, have you told anyone about that video?"

"No."

More silence.

"But what are we going to do about it, honey?" she whispered.

"Nothing. I've told you a million times. We cannot do anything. You do understand that, don't you?" He brushed her platinum blonde hair and kissed the top of her head.

"But—"

"The police do not need our help. I'm sure they'll discover the culprit without our being involved. It's one of their own men. They've probably already caught the person. We'll always just keep the video between us, remember?"

She said nothing.

"Fantasy?"

She finally nodded.

He lifted her chin and kissed her deeply. "Otherwise, there'll be no more of this." He kissed her again.

"I know. But …"

"No buts, my dear girl. Now, I have to go to work to earn the money that keeps you in this luxurious place. You do like living here, don't you?"

She nodded. "Yes."

"And driving your new car and shopping at the best

stores?"

She nodded.

"Good. Then you must abide by the rules. If you're a good girl, I was thinking we should go boating again. This time on my yacht up at the lake. Just us. I had such a wonderful time Saturday, except for what we need to forget about. Would you like that?"

"Oh, yes, I'd love that. I'd love to go on your yacht."

"Good. We'll go up to Lake Erie in the morning. No one will know us up there. We'll have much more freedom. We'll spend the weekend on the water. Tell your boss you're with your sick mother. I doubt they'll question it. You pack your things and I'll pick you up at nine in the morning." He smiled, got out of bed, went into the bathroom, and closed the door behind him.

The ceiling fan turned slowly above Fantasy. Talking about Lake Erie and the video had conjured up a memory of her and Joey Reed.

They were eating at Pier W in Cleveland. They talked and laughed as they watched the lights of the tiny boats on Lake Erie and the twinkling city to their north. They went back to a beautiful downtown hotel and got little sleep.

She knew he'd cared about her. He probably still did. She rolled over on her side and curled her hands under her chin. "That poor man," she whispered.

The shower turned on. She frowned and closed her eyes. "Poor, Joey," she whispered.

***

Emma pushed her cart around Weiland's, sipping a cup of lemonade the store offered to its customers. She shopped here because the staff was wonderful, the food was delicious, they had an amazing wine selection and liquor store, and it was two minutes from her condo.

She strolled through the wine section and laid a bottle of Côtes-du-Rhône in her cart. She needed groceries and a few pre-made items. Since Stratton wasn't around, she seldom cooked. She got a container of chicken salad from the cold deli and walked to the long cooler. She peered at the containers of premade meals. Everything looked good and she couldn't decide what to buy. She picked up a meal when her cell vibrated in her front pocket. She placed the container in her cart and strolled into an aisleway. She tapped the accept call icon and listened.

"You're sure?" she whispered.

"*Tak*. I saw with my own eyes. He pulled in the parking garage, and minutes later, they were kissing. I watched them through her window."

"Great work, Merek."

"I gotta scram," he said, and the call ended.

She tapped the face of her cell. Joey didn't answer. It rolled into his voicemail. In a low voice, she left a message. "Joey, it's me. I'll be there in a few minutes. It's important." She then called Janet and asked her to walk Millie. Janet was Charles's former neighbor and full-time dog walker. She walked his three rescued Labrador retrievers, referred to as "the boys" before he moved to Switzerland and her prior basset hound, Murray, who'd passed away.

She finished shopping, put her groceries away at home, then drove to the hospital to tell Joey the news.

***

The oak garage door rose and James Mars pulled the

black, twelve-year old Volvo into the garage, got out, and walked into the house. It was always great to have lunch with Cook and Sammy. They'd been friends for years. He missed being a cop.

He tossed the keys on the countertop and walked through the great room, out the sliding glass doors, and onto the patio. Dozens of birds squawked and fluttered around the empty bird feeders.

He took a deep breath. He was glad that Lieutenant Joey Reed was going to be okay. The police had no leads on the accident and were asking for information by calling a number, promising callers that tips would remain anonymous.

Joey had been to the house once to share a beer with his son in the family room, before the "updates." His wife, Lucy, wanted a "new look," and she certainly got it. He glanced toward the room and shuddered. He needed to redecorate. Or sell, although he knew he could never go through with either one.

He thought about his only child, Jimmy. It was hard to believe it had been seven years since he'd been shot in the line of duty. *Where had the time gone?*

And now, his Lucy—here but not. She had become a kind stranger who sometimes let his wife peek through. Her memory wavered—sometimes in midsentence. Conversations were often frustrating and it made him weary. But he visited her nearly every day at the Alzheimer's center, Sundays through Fridays. There were activities and several of Lucy's friends from the neighborhood, bridge club, and church members often visited her on Saturdays. She never mentioned missing him. He doubted she did.

He walked into the kitchen. His plate and cup looked lonely sitting in the drainer, and his mind flashed back to

Lucy and him standing at this sink doing dishes together while they listened to NPR or classical music or a Cleveland Indians game. Lucy loved washing dishes. He loathed it. But she rarely used the dishwasher, and it was together time for them in the evening after Jimmy went to bed.

He washed. She dried. One evening, she flipped him on the butt with the dish towel when Jimmy and his wife, Melissa, and their children, Joshua and Kasandra, were visiting. "Grandma! Why are you spanking Grandpa?" four-year old Joshua yelled as James jumped to get out of her way, chuckling. Lucy laughed that sing-song laugh of hers, explaining that Grandpa was ornery. *Oh, how I miss that laugh,* he thought.

He missed his family. He couldn't blame Melissa for remarrying several years after Jimmy died. But why did she have to move to Arizona and take their grandchildren so far away? All he ever wanted was a normal family. And he had one—at least for a little while. He had a beautiful wife, a son who followed in his father's footsteps as a police officer, a lovely daughter-in-law, and two perfect grandchildren. Now, they were all gone in one form or another.

He shuffled down the hall into the bedroom and put on his pajamas. As he buttoned the pajama top, he glanced in the closet and saw the shirt Lucy had bought him for Christmas several years ago. It was the family's last Christmas together. He smiled faintly at the memory of his grandchildren ripping through the presents, wrapping, bows, and laughter flying everywhere. Jimmy and Melissa sat on the couch, holding hands as everyone sipped eggnog and nibbled Lucy's Christmas cookies.

Lucy had handed him a wrapped box with a huge

yellow bow—her favorite color. It was the shirt he'd seen while they were on vacation in Colorado that summer. She made him try it on, and he came out of the dressing room to model it for her. She loved it, but he couldn't buy it. "It's such a loud color. It's not my style."

"Rubbish. It's the color of sunshine. It suits you," she said.

But none of it mattered anymore. Just memories, forever lost to Lucy and Jimmy. Sometimes he wished he could forget them, too. And Melissa simply didn't care anymore. She had a new life with a new husband, far away.

Maybe tomorrow would be a good day, but they were happening less often. Maybe tomorrow, she'd be Lucy. He never knew.

***

Emma ate a slice of Dante's pizza at her kitchen counter. She skimmed the Wednesday paper and spent the most time on her favorite section—the comics. Her cell buzzed next to her plate. She checked the screen and smiled.

"Charles. How are you?"

"Unfortunately, I'm not well, Emma. I have news, both good and bad."

Emma sat up in her chair. "What's wrong? What happened?"

"Father and I had to put Sam down yesterday. Cancer. He was simply becoming too uncomfortable. It was … heart wrenching."

"Oh, Charles, I'm sorry. I wish I could be there with you."

"I do, too. I'll call Janet later and inform her."

"I'm sorry, Charles," Emma said.

Charles began to sob. "I'm sorry," he blubbered. "It's just so ... difficult."

Emma glanced at Millie. "I know. How old was he?"

"He was approximately twelve," Charles choked.

"There's nothing I can say to take away your pain. He had the best years of his life with you. I'm so sorry." Emma began to cry but didn't want Charles to hear her.

She listened while Charles got a grip on himself, then he said, "I have additional news, as well."

"I hope it's good news," Emma said.

"Yes, it is. I'm retiring."

"What? That's great!" Emma yelled.

"Yes. I don't need to work. I've decided to, well, Emma, I'm coming home. Back to Clintonville. I want to become more involved with the Labrador rescue and the community. Sam's death made me realize I need to do more with my life. And I simply want to return home."

"You're leaving Switzerland and moving back here?" She jumped from her chair. Millie glanced at her and wagged her tail while she stood in front of her bowl, eating her food.

"Yes. As soon as I can find a suitable residence."

"This is the best news ever! I can't wait. Does Mary know?"

"No. I haven't informed her yet. But Father and I have decided to 'come out,' so to speak. We're going to tell Mother about the rekindling of our relationship and that he's been living with me. The entire truth."

"What? Wow! She will totally flip. I had dinner with her Monday."

"How is she?"

"Normal," Emma said.

"Drunk, you mean?" Charles asked.

Emma didn't answer the question. "I think she needs another man in her life to play with. That business with Devereux knocked that ole gal for a loop. She still talks about him. I think she really did love that Ponzi shyster."

"I agree. Mary would never admit it, but she wants to settle down," he said.

"Wait until she hears about you and your dad."

"Yes. That will be another blow to her already bruised ego, I'm sure. Once Father and I are settled, we are going to tell her together. I'd also like you to be there if you can. We may need your support."

"Or a referee." They laughed. "You can count on it. When will you be home?" she asked.

"This chalet will sell quickly. I've already talked to a realtor. Enough about me. How is Millie?"

"She's good. I'm getting ready to walk her in a few minutes. We're at home right now."

"Splendid. How's Stratton?"

She paused. "He's good."

"Wonderful. Listen, Emma, I have to run. We'll talk soon."

"Okay. Call me anytime," she said.

"Certainly. And Emma?"

"Yes?"

"I'm looking forward to coming home."

"I can't wait, either. Bye."

"Goodbye."

The call ended. Emma pumped her fist in the air. "Yes! Uncle Charles is coming home! He's coming home, baby girl!"

Millie ran in circles, barking, and wagging her tail.

***

Joey was certain that Fantasy had Brexton run over him in a boat, no matter the reason and how much Emma disagreed.

"First off, I don't think Fantasy is the type to have someone run over you. I don't think she's that ... smart or dumb or whatever. And like I keep asking you ... Why would they? If she wanted to get rid of you, there's easier ways to do it, all by herself. And, what's the point? Talk about no motive. She's obviously latched onto a very rich man. Nothing personal, but I think ole Brexie's done a little better than you in the money department, my much-lower-paid-police-Lieutenant friend. Why would she want to ruin her setup? What's his motive? Jealousy? Come on. Why would they care now? I still can't buy it," Emma kept telling him the same story.

He rolled their conversation over in his mind as he picked up his phone, set it back on the table and frowned. *What a mess,* he thought.

Edith, an older African-American nurse, walked into the room. She was Joey's favorite nurse out of all those who cared for him. She'd told him she and her husband were from Georgia. He was a cardiologist who'd been transferred to Columbus. They'd met while he was doing his residency.

Edith was a wise, kind, loving soul, who enjoyed helping people heal. She said she'd known since she was a little girl—patching up her dollies—that the lord wanted her to be a nurse, so she went to nursing school. "I always do what the lord tells me to do. And my gut."

"How you doing today, Mr. Reed?" she asked, checking his IV.

"I'm okay, I guess."

"You look like you're contemplating an escape. I wouldn't advise it."

"You ever known anyone to be jealous or angry enough that they would try to kill someone?" he asked.

"No. Can't say that I have. You're not jealous of me, are you? No reason to be. I have enough love to go around for all my patients. You don't need to be talking like this. Makes your blood pressure spike. You're my best patient, just like all the rest."

He laughed. "If I can't break out of here, when do I get discharged? I'm going crazy."

"I can't say, but everything is going well. You're healing up fine. You need to start moving around more. You can't just lay here all day. You'll get all squishy and mean. I'll be back. We'll get you into a wheelchair and go for another spin outside. I can leave you by the curb, and you can use Uber for an escape ride."

"I'm all for that," he said.

She patted his leg and left.

He lay back in his bed, thoughts whirling through his mind. *Brexton Birch, one of the biggest attorneys in town, risked his career—his life—to run over me with his boat. Fantasy is great in the sack, but how could he be that stupid?* But then again, he didn't really know Brexton, other than finding out a few things for him on a divorce case, years ago. He seemed like a level-headed attorney. But Merek saw what he saw and all things pointed to Brexton and Fantasy, no matter what Emma thought. It was time to talk to Fantasy himself.

He picked up his cell and tapped in a number from

memory. The call rolled into voice mail. "Fantasy, it's Joey. I need you to come by Riverside Hospital, room 402, right away. If I'm not here, wait until I get back. I need to talk to you. The sooner, the better."

***

"How's the divorce business these days?" Frank Long asked Brexton as he took another sip of wine.

"It's good," Brexton answered, putting his napkin aside.

"He's so busy, he's seldom home. And he has meetings every morning, away from the office. Don't you, dear?" Sheila said.

All eyes shifted to Brexton.

He flicked a look at Sheila, and she gave him a wicked smile. Brexton cleared his throat. "Yes. I thought it might be best to meet with my clients where they feel more comfortable or it's more convenient for them, instead of a stuffy law office. A new business model the firm is trying."

"Interesting," Frank replied. "You represent mostly women in these divorces. I can understand your new approach, I suppose. As long as you're, shall we say, careful."

Brexton looked at Frank. "I understand more than anyone. Lately, I've been meeting clients in a room at the courthouse. It's a more convenient location for them and it is a professionally public place, nicely decorated. I always bring one of our female lawyers with me, too." He smiled.

"After all, it is all about serving the client, isn't it dear?" Sheila said.

A tense quiet energy filled the Birch's dining room.

"Sheila, the centerpiece is divine. Did you arrange it yourself?" Wilma Long, Frank's wife, nearly shouted as she cut another piece of steak and shoved it into her mouth.

She chews like a cow, Sheila thought as she answered. "Oh, dear me, no. I have a professional flower arranger do all my bouquets once a week. He does a superb job. I can give you his name, if you like. They only charge six hundred dollars for an arrangement like this. I have one in nearly every room. Brexton loves them, don't you, dear?"

Brexton nodded without looking at his wife. "I pay for them, don't I?"

Wilma gave Sheila a thin smile and washed her steak down with a gulp of wine.

"Have you been doing any fishing lately?" Frank asked Brexton.

"No, but it's funny you mention it. I'm driving up to Lake Erie in the morning and taking a client out on the yacht. I'll be there through the weekend. We're going to fish while we discuss a large real estate deal. He's an avid fisherman, and as my wife pointed out, it is all about serving the client."

"You didn't mention this to me," Shelia said, putting down her wine glass with a thud.

"Why should I? It's business. It's only the weekend. Besides, I got you two tickets to see *Hamilton* Saturday night. A surprise. You can take one of your friends or a peer from the hospital board." He nearly winced as he said it. He paid more for those tickets than he paid for his monthly expenses. Anything to keep Sheila occupied.

"Well, isn't that sweet? What a darling husband I

have, don't you think?" Sheila asked their guests.

"Those tickets are hard to come by. How'd you do it?" Frank asked.

"Let's just say I have my connections and leave it at that. Now, let's move into the parlor for dessert. We'll be having a specially made cake, right dear?" Brexton said.

"Why, yes. Thank you for finding the time to pick it up for me," Sheila said.

"It wasn't a problem. No problem at all," he said as he stood. "Please, after you." He gestured their guests toward the hallway.

Sheila fiddled with the cell in her pocket and glanced at it. It wasn't her normal phone, but one she had purchased to talk with one person only. Brexton never noticed the difference. "Excuse me. I have to make a call."

She walked into the study, shut the door, set her glass of wine on a table, and walked to a far corner of the room. She pulled the phone from her pocket and hit a send call key.

The call was accepted, but there was no answer on the other end.

"He's going to Lake Erie tomorrow morning. He'll be taking our yacht You know where it is. He's likely taking her with him. This is even better." She paused. "No, just him. Make *her* take the blame. You know what to do." She ended the call, smoothed her dress, and walked back to Brexton and their guests.

Thursday

AT EIGHT O'CLOCK on Thursday morning, there was a tap on the door. Joey expected it was Emma with breakfast.

"I got your message. Can I come in?" Fantasy asked.

Joey's cell was on the hospital table in front of him. He hit the audio record button. As Edith would say, "You gotta listen to your gut." His gut told him to do it.

"Come on in."

She walked into the room as if she were approaching a tiger. She pulled the orange chair from the wall and turned it to face him before she sat down. She was dressed in a short skirt and her hair and makeup were perfect—as always. She crossed her tanned legs and gave Joey a sad smile.

"I'm so sorry, Joey. You poor thing. I can only stay a couple of minutes, but thought I'd drop by as soon as I could after I got your message."

"We need to talk," Joey said flatly.

Fantasy gave him a serious nod. "Okay." *He's going to tell me he still loves me*, she thought.

"How did you find out about my accident?" he asked. He watched her closely.

"That obnoxious friend of yours, Emma. She came to my place and told me. She wasn't very nice to me. She was insulting. In fact, it was like she was blaming me or something. I'd like it if you would talk to her. She's very rude. Then Merek came by. I'd appreciate if you'd tell them both to leave me alone."

Joey held her look in silence. She squirmed in the chair.

"Joey? Don't look at me like that. What's wrong?" she said, placing a hand on his arm.

"What do you think?"

"What do you mean?" She pulled her hand away.

"Come on, Fantasy. Cut the shit."

"What are you talking about?"

"Look, I know you're involved with my being here somehow, but I just don't know how—yet. But I will find out."

"What are you talking about? I don't have anything to do with anything. I only came here because you asked me to." Her voice rose and she put a hand to her throat. "What are you talking about?"

Edith walked into the room and stood behind Fantasy. "Everything all right here, Mr. Reed? Your blood pressure and heart beat just spiked up on my monitor," she said as she frowned at the top of Fantasy's bleached head.

"Yes, Edith. My friend is just exasperated to see me like this. Aren't you?" He nearly gritted his teeth as he looked at his visitor.

"You sure everything's okay?" Edith asked again. "It's way before normal visiting hours."

"It's not a problem. Thanks for coming by," Joey said, not taking his eyes off Fantasy's.

"Okay, but I'm coming back in a few minutes," Edith said.

"Thanks, Edith. My guest will be leaving soon."

Edith left with her hands on her hips.

"Anything you want to tell me, you'd best tell me now. Because if you don't, I'll find out anyway. I knew you were pissed when we split, but I didn't think you could talk Brexton Birch into running over me with his boat," Joey said.

Fantasy shot out of the chair and leaned over Joey. "I don't know anything about what you're talking about. Brexton didn't run over you," she shouted. "I mean, I don't even know anyone named Brexton Birch."

"Save it, Fantasy. I know you're seeing him."

Fantasy slowly sat in the chair, deflated. "Joey, please. I'll tell you anything. Just don't get Brexton involved. Please. Please. It would ruin him. He would hate me. I'll do anything. Just don't tell him."

"Well, he certainly tried to ruin me, now didn't he? Excuse me, but he's already involved."

"He didn't do this. I *know* he didn't," she squeaked.

"And just how do you *know*?"

Tears welled in her eyes, and she fumbled with her purse strap. "First, promise me that you'll never talk to Brexton. Promise me."

"I'm sorry, Fantasy. But attempted murder is a little bit against the law. And I am a cop. Remember?"

"Joey, please. I know he didn't do it. I can get proof he didn't do it."

"Proof? What, your word? You've got to be kidding me."

A tear rolled down her cheek. "I can show you a video of who did it. It wasn't him."

Joey looked at her. "I'm listening."

Fantasy told him about Brexton's video. "You can't see anything except a speedboat going toward a blue dot in the water and then white splashes and the boat taking off. That's all you can see, I swear. That helicopter camera thing was up too high. The drone. If I get the video for you, please, promise you won't tell Brexton or get him involved."

Joey gave her a long look.

"Joey, please," she begged. "I need some time. But I'll get it."

He continued to stare at her. A wave of pity and disgust washed over him. "I'll get the video with or without you, Fantasy. It's evidence."

"Joey, please. Just give me a little time. It'll take me awhile to get the video without him knowing about it, but I'll get it. I just need a little time. I promise. Don't get Brexton involved. You owe me that much."

"You're a real piece of work, you know that?"

Fantasy jumped from the chair and ran out of the room. Joey turned off the audio recorder on his phone and called Miles.

As he was ending the call, Edith walked back into the room. She stood at the foot of the bed with both hands on her hips and raised eyebrows. "Mr. Reed, you shouldn't be having visitors that make you upset. Your face is flushed."

"I'm fine," he said.

"Who do you think you're talking to? My, mercy." There was a rap on the open door.

"I know you have McDonald's for him—again. Do you people think nurses are naïve? You can smell that stuff for miles. We see this all the time, especially when our patients have diet restrictions. But since Mr. Reed has no restrictions, it's okay. It must make him happy as many wrappers as I see coming out in his trash bag. Oh, yes. I sure do check my patient's trash. I don't want them doing anything behind my back. But you can only bring that stuff in here if you brought me something, too," she said with a wide grin.

"As a matter of fact, I got two extra Egg McMuffins in case you were hungry. And an extra coffee," Emma said.

"Well, that's more like it," Edith said. "But I can't eat another bite. I had a *healthy* breakfast at home and some of us have to work. But I will take that coffee." She grabbed a cup from the holder as she made her way out of the room.

***

Sheila Birch gazed out the window with a look on her face as if she were standing in the sun after weeks of rain.

A young maid walked into the den with a tray of coffee and a rose in a sterling silver vase that sat beside a warm breakfast under a silver cover. The ensemble was an anniversary gift Brexton gave to Sheila years ago so they could have more breakfasts in bed. The Thursday morning issue of *The Columbus Dispatch* was folded neatly on the side.

"Set it there," Sheila ordered the young maid.

"Yes, ma'am."

"I'm sorry," Sheila said, turning from the window. "I was thinking of something else. What's your name?"

"Lori, ma'am."

"Lori. May I ask what brought you to us? I don't remember you or even hiring a new employee."

Lori blushed. "Mr. Birch told me to apply. He helped my former employer with her divorce, and I didn't want to work for the woman anymore. When I met your husband once, he said for me to apply with him. So I did."

Lori was young, maybe in her thirties. She was also beautiful without a drop of makeup and sweet in a plain kind of way. Sheila suspected Brexton was probably sleeping with her and having her close made it easier. Her face turned crimson and she took a deep breath.

"That will be all, Lori. You can leave the premises. We won't be needing your services any longer."

"But ... Have I done something wrong?"

"It would be best for you to leave," Sheila said.

Lori took a step back, dumbfounded.

"Now," Sheila said. "I'll make sure you're paid for your time. I'm sure Brexton had your address somewhere that I can find. Better yet, jot it down and leave it on the kitchen counter before you go."

"But . . . Can I talk with Mr. Birch? I really need this job. And I wanted to work for him. He was so kind to me."

"Yes, I'm sure he was." She raised her chin defiantly. "Mr. Birch won't be returning for some time. He's on a *long* business trip. A very long business trip. Now, get out of my house."

Lori turned like a zombie and walked out of the room.

Sheila sat on the couch. She uncovered her breakfast and began to eat, savoring every delicious bite until there was a knock at the door. It was the police.

***

Emma and Joey had finished their breakfast and were still talking when Joey's cell buzzed.

"Miles. Yeah. I see. That's what Sheila Birch said? And Fantasy's car's in the garage but she's not home or at work? And he left earlier this morning? I see." He and Emma looked at each other while he talked. "Yeah. Yeah. I think they are, too. Call the highway patrol and Cleveland PD and the Coast Guard. Hopefully, we can catch them before they get on his boat." He ended the call and put the phone back on the table.

"Brexton Birch is going to be on his yacht in Lake Erie this weekend with a so-called fisherman, discussing a business deal. That's the story that Sheila Birch gave Miles. She didn't know anything more. Birchie isn't answering his calls. He, and likely Fantasy, are driving up 71 on their way to Cleveland right now. Anyway, like I said, Fantasy told me about this video taken from a drone and wanted me to give her time to get it without Brexton knowing." He shook his head and took a drink of coffee.

"That's got to be the drone in Bobby's video. You can barely see it, but your guys confirmed it was a drone, but they couldn't make out anything more. I don't think Fantasy girl is lying this time. If they didn't do it, which I never thought they did, maybe we can see who did on Brexton's video. Talk about a weird coincidence. What are the odds? But she did know you were out there, thanks to you. I guess we'll see." She gave him a sarcastic grin.

"I can't believe he's stupid enough to have a fling with someone like her," Joey said.

"That doesn't say much for you and Merek."

125

"Yeah, whatever. You know what I mean. Birch is a popular, hot shot divorce lawyer who represents women whose husbands are cheating on them. It's just nuts. Fantasy has her strengths, don't get me wrong, but—"

"But you wouldn't think a guy like Birch would risk his entire life for her. I didn't, either. I was stunned when Merek called me, to be honest. But stranger things happen every day. You know that. I guess it's like kids who wear shoes have no cobblers, as Merek would say."

Joey nodded and grinned.

Emma pulled her cell out of her purse and hit a number on her speed dial. "Merek, we're taking a trip north to Lake Erie. I'll be there to pick you up in twenty." She waited a moment before she ended the call. "He had to scram," she said, putting her phone back in her purse.

"Emma, I know you're trying to help and you feel responsible and all, but we need to handle this from here. Don't go."

"Are you kidding? I'm going to be there when they pull Brexton and Fantasy off that boat."

"Seriously. Don't go," Joey said.

Emma glared at him and crossed her arms in front of her.

Joey picked up his phone and hit the screen. "Miles? Yeah. Listen, I want you take Emma and Merek with you on the boat. They'll meet you at the marina. And take Matt, just in case you need him. I have a funny feeling about this." He listened. "Yeah. No. Yeah. I don't think it's intended to be a ride on the Love Boat, but she probably doesn't know that." He listened. "Yeah, that's what I think, too. Just keep it from getting out of control and get that video." He ended the call.

He and Emma looked at each other and said in

unison, "He's going to throw her overboard."

***

Fantasy leaned across the console of the BMW loaner car and kissed Brexton on the cheek. Earlier, he dropped off his car at the dealership to get an oil change and tune-up. He told them he would pick it up on Sunday afternoon. Although he doubted anyone would be looking for him, they'd likely be looking for his car, and this was simply a precaution.

"I'm so excited. I can't wait to get on that big boat. I've never stayed overnight on the water."

They sped past the exit for Medina. He glanced at the clock. They were making good time. He was glad Fantasy was punctual, unlike Sheila.

"I tried to call you earlier. Where were you?"

"Oh, you did? I must've been in the shower. I'm sorry." She looked out the side window.

Brexton said nothing. They traveled. Both were lost in their own thoughts.

"You left both your phones in your apartment, right?" he asked.

She nodded. "Yes, but I still don't understand why you told me to do that."

"There's no reason to bring them. There's no reception on the lake," he lied. "No phones. No calls. No texts. And, definitely—*no videos*. This is *our* weekend, sweetheart. Just me and you. No one but us. That's all. We'll set off then have lunch, which will be on the boat by the time we board—complete with several bottles of Dom Perignon. Maybe we can play a round of putt-putt at Put-In-Bay. I'll even let you win." He winked at her.

He had prepaid in cash for the account and phones just for them when they started seeing each other, making them virtually impossible to track. As he drove, he pondered on the best way to destroy the phones later. He left his phone at the office.

Fantasy watched the landscape scroll by, wondering how she was going to get her hands on the video. She couldn't get into his house. Was it at his office? Still on his speedboat? Had it been on his phone or a little camera? She couldn't remember. But she had to get that video somehow and give it to Joey. Soon. When the time was right, she'd ask Brexton about it—again—or maybe just ask about drones in general. No matter how she approached it, she had to be careful. She dreaded the thought.

He reached over and patted her thigh. She jumped.

"Why so jumpy?"

"I'm just excited," she said.

"I understand. I want us both to simply enjoy our time together."

She studied her frowning reflection in the side window. He hadn't brought the drone. She wasn't surprised. She had to keep her cool. A few minutes passed before she sat back in the soft leather seat, raised her arms above her head, stretched, and put on a big smile. "My life is almost everything I ever wanted it to be, since I met you."

"Almost?" he asked.

"You know what I mean."

"I told you the rules going into this," he said.

"Let's not talk about it. I want us to enjoy our time together, too, since we don't get that much of it. This is so exciting, honey." She wrapped herself around his arm and laid her head on his shoulder. While she grew tired of being the "other woman," she would play by his rules—for now.

"Yes, it is. I'm looking forward to really relaxing, do a little fishing. It'll be just you and me out on that big, beautiful lake. I checked the weather and it's in our favor." He grinned.

Fantasy clapped her hands like a child. "You're so wonderful, Brex."

"I agree."

They arrived at the BigC Marina in Cleveland in record time and parked in the back of the lot. He would board the yacht. She would wait, and then nonchalantly walk down the boardwalk, as if she were a tourist admiring the boats, making sure no one was watching before she got on the yacht in the last slip on the right along the dock.

Brexton gave her a peck on the cheek, got out of the car, and removed a small suitcase with their belongings and his briefcase from the trunk. He opened the door and handed her the keys. He strolled through the parking lot to a small glass-windowed office on the dock. The man inside waved and slid the window to the side. They talked, and Brexton threw back his head in laughter.

Fantasy loved to watch him. His every move made her heart soar. She didn't get many opportunities to see him interact with people. Except the other day at the restaurant. He said it was Sheila's idea and he couldn't say no. He told her he was proud of her for how she acted in the situation. Someday, they would be together and he'd be all hers. She knew it.

The man came out of the building, still talking to Brexton. He patted the man on the shoulder, and they shook hands. The man left the office and walked the other direction, and Brexton continued down the dock.

Fantasy waited. A line of sweat appeared above her lip. She wiped it off, checked her face in the mirror, and reapplied her lipstick. She waited a few more seconds before she got out of the car and locked it with the fob. The car tweeted and blinked as if to say "Have a wonderful trip." She headed toward the dock. She was glad the man had left the office. She saw no one as she sashayed down the wooden planks. Gulls squawked overhead and the water sparkled. She breathed in the clean air as she stopped to admire the boats. These weren't boats, these were yachts like the ones she'd seen on TV.

Finally, she came to the end of the dock. She looked up at the three-story yacht. "Wow," she said.

As she climbed aboard the *Esquire Too*, her cell phone on the nightstand in Clintonville flashed and buzzed with voicemail and text notifications.

***

James Mars pulled his Volvo into the parking lot at the Alzheimer's center. He looked at the building for several seconds, got out of the car, and trudged up the sidewalk.

"Hello, James. How are you today?" the desk clerk greeted him.

"Fine. Fine, thank you. I believe I have a date with my beautiful wife for lunch," he said.

"You certainly do. I'm sure she's ready and waiting," she replied, smiling.

"Thank you, Becky."

She nodded as she picked up the ringing telephone.

James walked into the dining area, where he spotted Lucy sitting at their regular table. She wore a bright pink sweater and was chatting with two women at the next table. James sat down across from her.

"There he is. I told you he'd be here soon. Ladies, this is my husband, James."

Greetings were exchanged before Lucy turned her attention to him.

"Hi, honey. How are you today?"

He felt a lift in spirit. "I'm fine, sweetheart. How are you?"

"Splendid. Just splendid. The women and I were just talking about knitting. Do you remember all those booties I knitted for Jimmy? Oh, dear," she chuckled and waved a hand. "None of them ever fit. He kicked them off as soon as I put them on his little feet. Do you remember?"

"I do." *Maybe his Lucy would stay here for a while*, he thought.

"Well, mothers do those sorts of things, you know. I never did get the knack for knitting. I ended up buying him booties instead. He didn't seem to mind, but he didn't wear those, either." She patted his hand. "Anyway, what shall we have for lunch today? I'm up for something fun and different."

James looked at her, praying this would last. This was his Lucy. The woman he loved. "I don't know. What are you in the mood for, dear?"

"I guess we'll just have to see what the specials are today." She winked at him and grabbed his hand. "How goes it at home?"

"Fine. Fine. I fed the birds," he said.

"Oh, I'm so glad. You need to feed them every morning and evening. Otherwise, they get fussy." She turned around in her chair, scanning the room. "Where is she?"

"Who, honey?" he asked.

"Melissa. She said she'd be bringing our lunches."

His heart sank. How could this be happening? He took a deep breath and felt the weight of a building fall on him—again. "I'm sure she'll be by soon." He squeezed her hand.

"When I talked to her last night, she said she would bring us lunch. And Jimmy may stop by later, when he gets off duty. He works so many hours. But I'm so proud of him, following in his father's footsteps. I hope one of them bring the babies. He's such a fine police officer. Such a fine man." She beamed and patted his hand. "Just like his father. I wish you knew them. I'm sorry. What's your name again?"

"My name is James. James Mars," he said sadly.

***

Merek leaned on a post along the dock of the BigC Marina. Emma paced as Miles talked with a man inside a small glass-windowed office. After several minutes, Miles came out and addressed Matt, two local police officers, and two men with the Coast Guard. Emma and Merek stood behind them.

Miles looked at his watch. "The manager said he talked with Brexton Birch here about eleven thirty this morning. He didn't mention where he was going, but he said Birch told him he was meeting a client in Toledo and they were going to be doing some fishing.

"He left here and got on his boat. He was alone. The man said he didn't see anyone else, but he did leave his office immediately to go eat lunch after he talked to

Birch. He also forgot his cell phone. He left it at home this morning, so when your shop called, he didn't get the message," he looked at one of the local officers.

"We got here as fast as we could," the officer said to Miles. "We had an 11-71. It was a huge warehouse."

"Birch is not answering his radio. Chopper is scanning the water right now and everyone's been notified," one of the Coast Guardsmen said.

"I'm going out. You can come with us," an officer said to Matt and Miles. Emma cleared her throat.

"These two need to come along. They're helping Reed with the investigation," Miles said.

The local officers gave Emma and Merek the once-over. "Just stay out of the way," one of them said.

Matt went to the Clintonville cruiser and retrieved his rifle case, threw it over his shoulder, and walked toward Emma and Merek. "You two should really stay here," he said to them.

"I am staying. I am not going on the boat," Merek said. "I must stay on the land. All of you, be safe."

"We will," Emma said before she, Miles, and Matt boarded the police boat.

Everyone put on bulletproof vests under their life jackets. As the police boat motored out into the open water beside the Coast Guard boat, Emma and Merek waved to each other. He loved looking at water, but could never be on it or in it again. Not since one of his brothers pushed him off his uncle's small boat into a lake in Poland when they were young. Even though he had on a life jacket, Merek couldn't swim and it terrified him.

Voices crackled over a radio and on the shoulder speakers of the officers. The boats launched into top speed. The *Esquire Two* had been seen moving west with two passengers at a high rate of speed.

Emma sat down. Matt sat beside her. "Looks like they're both still on the yacht," he yelled toward her. "That's a good thing."

Emma nodded. "As long as we get there before Birch tries anything."

***

"We've been going fast for a long time, Brex. Can we stop? Please? I want to stop for a while. When will we be at the islands so we can walk around and hold hands like a real couple? You said we could do that," Fantasy whined. She wore only one of his dress shirts that made a mini dress for her. She stood against Brexton who was driving the boat in the air-conditioned flybridge. She watched him, looked at the controls on the dash, and sipped champagne.

He wore a pair of Nike swim trunks and flip flops. He lowered a small pair of binoculars that hung around his neck. He saw no boats to be concerned about. He slowed the yacht to a stop and it floated on the water.

"Change of plans, my sweet. We're not going to the islands. We're heading to Toledo. Bigger crowds and I'd like to go to the art museum. I'd like to see the Degas exhibit." *And deeper water*, he thought.

"Deeegauz? What's that? I have never been to an art museum." She giggled.

"You'll love it. That's all you need to know. Don't you worry that gorgeous little head of yours. I'm here to take care of everything. This is our time. Let's go up on deck for a little while."

She took another sip from her drink, set the glass

down, and followed him. They leaned on the bow railing and gazed out over the lake. "This is wonderful, Brex," she said.

"Yes, except the wind is picking up a bit," he said.

***

The police boat smacked over the whitecaps as it zoomed along beside the Coast Guard boat. Matt walked to the bow. He was tired. He got to bed late and hadn't slept well. He was fighting a summer cold. A cough or sneeze at the wrong time could be hazardous if his services were needed.

He squeezed his eyes shut, remembering that moment in the desert. He'd been shaky from drinking too much the night before and sneezed. It cost his buddy's life. He never touched another drop of alcohol.

He turned his thoughts to better things—his wife and two kids and the fun they'd had Saturday night. They had all gone to a local pub for dinner and "family night." The kids played games with the staff while he and his wife snuggled together, holding hands. She sipped a local brew, and he drank a Pepsi. They watched their kids win at a ball-throwing game and his heart soared as he remembered the smiles on everyone's faces. After they dropped the kids off at her mother's, he and his wife went home and enjoyed a quiet evening.

Now he needed to focus. Although he knew this would not be anything like what he dealt with during the war, the thought of shooting the most popular attorney in town made his stomach churn.

He sipped a bottle of water and listened to the monitor on his shoulder. He wondered why Brexton Birch would think he could get away with killing anyone. *People are so stupid,* he thought. But he was told Birch's possible plan was to kill his lover and throw the body in the lake, and his job was to help not let that happen—if he could.

He glanced at Emma. He knew that she and Joey had worked together for years, but who was the big, tattooed, pierced guy they'd left behind? He didn't really care. He knew his job, and it was never to worry about the past or future or things that didn't concern him.

Matt could hit anything. He'd been shooting rocks off a ledge at his dad's farm since he could walk. And he got better and better the farther away his dad made him stand. But he didn't care to shoot from boats. And these whitecaps wouldn't help. He preferred shooting from a tripod on solid ground. But he certainly wouldn't shoot anyone if he didn't have to.

Finally, the police and Coast Guard boats came up fast from behind the yacht's stern, making their way to its port side. There was talk on the radio, and an officer pointed. Matt followed the direction of his finger. He disappeared like a panther. The boats stopped, rolling on whitecaps, the wind pushing them toward the bow of the yacht on the port side.

***

Emma glanced up at the top deck of the boat. The tip of Matt's rifle peeked out over the edge. She cinched her bulletproof vest tighter and moved to the gunwale of the police boat where she was instructed to sit.

Birch and Fantasy leaned against the top railing on the port side, near the bow of the yacht.

"Brex—" A loud pop and a ping interrupted the

Coast Guard announcer and Birch and Fantasy hit the deck. So did everyone else.

"What's going on?" Fantasy screamed at Brexton as he dropped to the deck floor. She lay down beside him.

"I have no idea. Someone is obviously trying to kill us, you idiot. Oh, this is horrible. I should've gotten rid of you a long time ago. This is all your fault, you worthless slut," he yelled.

"What did you say?" she yelled back.

"Nothing!"

"Why is the Coast Guard shooting at us?" she screamed.

"How the hell should I know?"

They belly-crawled, making their way toward the middle of the yacht. He was on the edge, nearest the water. She stopped and rolled on her side to face him. "I heard what you said."

"Shut up!" he yelled.

She gave him a disgusted look, then pushed him hard. He rolled off the side of the yacht and splashed into the lake. She peered over the edge.

***

Matt had Birch in his sight. He didn't appear armed. In fact, he looked relaxed as he leaned on the railing, standing beside a woman. Her waist-long blonde hair lifted in the breeze, and she wore an oversized men's dress shirt.

He started to lower his rifle when he saw a slight movement in his peripheral vision to the left of the yacht and heard a shot. Birch fell onto the deck of the yacht, followed by the woman. Matt quickly moved his sight and spotted a man on his stomach on a small, black speedboat that was being pushed by the wind toward the bow of Brexton's yacht on the starboard side. A shooter was aiming at the yacht.

Matt spoke into his shoulder microphone, waited a split second for the reply, and squeezed the trigger.

A body rolled over the side of the black speedboat and made a small splash in the water. The Coast Guard boat quickly made its way there.

***

Brexton floundered in the water like a child. "Heeeelp," he squealed before he sunk down. Back up. "Can't ..." Down. Back up, gasping for air. Down. Up. "Hellll ..." Down. Up. Down. Not back up.

Fantasy watched for several seconds before she stood, peeled off Brexton's shirt, and tossed it on the deck. She dived naked into the water. She grabbed Brexton from behind and swam toward a police boat. He flopped and splashed as he gasped for breath.

"Calm down or I'll let you drown, you skunk. I can't believe you can't swim," she yelled in his ear.

He didn't answer and stopped flailing.

The police officers helped Fantasy and Brexton aboard the boat. Fantasy's lean legs went up to her ears as she climbed the ladder. She had a rock-solid, beautiful body. Officers draped blankets around her and Birch. She smoothed her hair and pulled the blanket around herself. An officer led a dripping Brexton Birch away from Fantasy. Birch was thanking the officer for showing up when they did, blubbering that someone was shooting at him and his client.

She looks like a Playboy model on a marketing shoot, Emma

thought as Fantasy walked toward her.

"I used to swim in the lake at my aunt's house. She taught me lifesaving. I never thought I'd have to use it," she said to Emma as she sat down and pulled the blanket tighter. "And just for the record, I'm not his client," she muttered.

Matt appeared from nowhere and sat beside Emma. "Good shot," she whispered in his ear.

Matt said nothing as he watched the Coast Guard board the black speedboat.

Fantasy raised her head and gave Emma a smirk. "Sorry I lied to you," she said.

Emma looked at her for a long moment. "Can I get you some water?" she asked.

"Thanks. That'd be great."

***

"I intend to keep traveling. I may be nearly eighty, but I'm still the best senior women's golfer in the world," Mary Wellington said to Samuel Jones.

"That's what I've read in the papers back home. I also saw you on the cover of several golfing magazines at the newsstand," Samuel said. He took his stance and hit the ball. He knew as soon as the club struck the ball that Mary had made the better shot. Typical. She was a natural-born golfer. He was never good, but he enjoyed playing a game now and then.

"How's Charles? He was such a wonderful student. I loved tutoring him. How long has it been? Over fifty years ago," he said as he climbed behind the wheel of the golf cart.

They careened toward their next play. She got off the

cart, chose an iron, and approached the ball. Her shot rolled near the hole. "He's perfect, I suppose, although how would I know? He totally ignores me. And all I wanted was to be a mother, at least once. I wanted him to marry and have children. But Charles has no interest in adopting. Well, it's all probably for the best, I suppose. But I would love it if he found a nice man, married, and adopted a child."

"I didn't realize Charles was gay or that you wanted to bounce grandbabies on your knee, Mary. My, my. You never struck me as the type all those years ago. But people change, I suppose. What surprises we learn about our friends and former lovers after time passes." He got off the cart, went to chip the ball and missed. He swore under his breath as Mary's lip curled slightly.

Later that evening, they sat on Mary's enclosed sun porch and watched the sunset over Circleville, Ohio.

"Are you seeing anyone?" Mary asked as she sipped her second martini.

He shook his head. "Is that why you asked me to come?" he asked.

She grinned. "Perhaps. You know, I always loved that British accent of yours, Samuel. And we had a wonderful time together when you were living here as Charles's tutor." She winked at him and sipped her drink. "John makes the best martinis on the planet. I know, I've drunk them all around the world. They keep me young."

"Alcohol is not to my liking. I'll stick to my tea," he said, raising his mug.

"You always were such a gentleman. Always sipping your tea." She reached over and took his hand. "And you're still so handsome. I'm glad you could come for a visit."

"And what about you? Anyone special in your life?" he asked.

She paused. "I came close to marriage. So close. A horrid creature named Devereux."

"Oh, yes, yes. That movie producer. I read about that, too. What a wedding that must have been. I'm so sorry."

The sky grew pink as they sat in silence with their thoughts.

After several minutes, Samuel said, "You need to move on, Mary. Find someone new. Someone you can travel and enjoy the rest of your life with. Someone to love."

Her eyes twinkled as she turned to him. "I do want to get married and have a trusted companion."

Friday

IT WAS ANOTHER hot morning. Joey sat reading in a chair. He turned to see Emma and Merek standing in his doorway. "Hey, guys. Come on in. Oh, good, you brought me some grub."

Emma held up a McDonald's bag. "Sure did." She and Merek went into the room. Merek leaned against a wall and sipped his CrimsonCup coffee.

Emma spread the food on the hospital table and rolled it in front of Joey. His arm and leg were both in new flexible casts.

"I can't thank you guys enough for going up there yesterday, even though you shouldn't have" Joey said. He lay the papers he was reading on the bed.

"There was a lot of action, that's for sure," Emma said. "I was really glad to get home last night. Needless to say, I didn't sleep much."

"Yeah, I was just reading over the preliminary report that Miles dropped off last night." Joey picked up the Egg McMuffin and took a huge bite. He moaned with satisfaction.

Emma sat down in the orange plastic chair and

picked up her coffee. "Maybe that's why you never settled down," she said.

"What?" Joey said with a full mouth.

"That." She pointed at his mouth, "That noise you make when you eat. What woman would want to live with that?"

He scowled at her, took another bite and moaned louder. They laughed.

"Looks like you are healing, Mr. Joey. You have new casts and you are not in bed," Merek said.

Joey raised his arm. "Sure am. This one is a lot more comfortable, and I can move now. And my leg has healed much faster than expected. Won't be long and I'll be outta this joint."

"That is good news," Merek said.

"Edith will have a fit if she sees you eating that stuff, you know," Emma said.

Joey nodded and glanced at Merek. "Did you already eat, my man?" Joey asked.

"I ate pierogies and sausage for breakfast today. I do not eat McDonald's."

"Good for you," Joey said, chasing his food with a sip of coffee. "You make good pierogies. I wouldn't mind having them again."

"I will bring you pierogies. Do you still not know who did this to you?" Merek asked.

Joey shook his head. "No. But now I know Birch and Fantasy didn't do it. The video that Fantasy told me about was still on the camera on the drone. They found it when they searched Birch's office. Ole Birchie Boy thought he deleted it, but he hadn't. Bad boy. Withholding evidence. You'd think he'd know better. He swore he never watched it and had no clue what was on it. But

Fantasy remembered what was on it pretty well." Joey smiled and took another bite.

"Did the video show anything that could help us find out who *did* run over you?" Emma asked.

"Glad you asked. Miles sent it to me and there is a new clue. The Bimini on the boat looks like it has white spots on the top of it, and it does appear the boat veered for me and took off. The view went low then lifted and then it went off camera pretty quick. Can't see more of the boat or where it went."

"White spots on the top? Hmmm. That is something new," she said.

"We sure couldn't see the top of that Bimini from water level," Joey said. "So getting that video was a good thing. Anyway, Fantasy can't *prove* Birch intended to off her on the boat and I don't think she believes that was his plan. And if she did file charges, it'd just be her word against his. It would never fly with his reputation. Oddly, Sheila Birch is going to get the brunt of all this. The guy that Matt picked off into the lake is a known hit man. Sheila hired him to nail Birch and make it look like Fantasy did it somehow. Anyway, he's been wanted for a long time, so that was an extra bennie in all this. Great timing. He was on the other side of the yacht and didn't see the cop or guard boats. He bargained and ratted out Sheila and several others. She broke down and confessed.

"I tried to warn Fantasy not to get on Birch's yacht. I called. I texted. Everything's on her phone. Birch told her to leave both her cell phones at her place. She pays for one in her name and he paid cash for the other one with prepaid minutes. That way, he'd be sure to have them both when he got back and there was no way she could call or we could track the phones while they were on the lake. He'd left his cell at his office. And him switching cars was a pretty good move.

"Not sure how he intended to kill her, they didn't find a weapon on the boat. But it doesn't matter. It didn't happen and he'll likely be divorcing his wife. She's going to need a good attorney."

"How ironic," Emma said with a laugh.

Joey looked at Merek. "Seems I wasn't the only one trying to warn Fantasy about Birch either."

Merek shrugged and sipped his coffee. "Her life was in danger. It was the thing to do," he said.

Joey nodded. "You are right, my Polish friend."

Joey turned to Emma. "Go ahead. Say it."

"Say what?" She drank her coffee.

"You didn't think Birch and Fantasy ran over me the entire time and I didn't listen. How were you so sure?"

She shrugged. "Gut feeling."

"You and Edith and your gut feelings. I think I just wanted it to be them or something, you know? And everything was pointing to them," Joey said.

"Sort of. But I never thought there was much motive there. She had too sweet of a deal going with Birch," she said.

"What are your thoughts about all this, Merek?" Joey asked.

He scratched his head and looked at the floor. The fluorescent lighting cast a glow on his tattoos and reflected off his earrings. "I will go back to the marinas and talk to different people."

Joey nodded. "Can't hurt. I'll have some of my guys on it, too."

Emma glanced at Joey's side table. It was piled with books, magazines, and papers. The list of registered boats was on the top of the stack. "Have you been looking over the list again?" she asked.

"Yeah, I glanced through it again this morning. There was a name on there that caught my eye the first time I looked at it. Never thought about it much when I saw it before."

"Who would that be, Mr. Joey?" Merek asked.

"James Mars. His son, Jimmy, and I were on the force together for a short time. He was fatally shot during a domestic. Very sad. He and his dad were both good cops. I never knew either of them, really. James was at another precinct and retired several years back. I remember they had a boat and lived on the lake. I was at their house for a beer once. Jimmy was their only kid." Joey frowned.

"Wait. I met James Mars this week," Emma said.

"What? You never mentioned it," Joey said.

"I never knew that I should. He stopped in to visit Cook and Sammy when I was there talking to them."

"Doesn't surprise me. They're friends. Not sure if his wife's still around. I didn't really know him but always heard good things about him. I don't even remember what the man looks like."

Emma sat back and crossed her arms.

"What?" Joey asked her.

"I don't know. This James Mars thing."

Joey gave her a sour look. "James Mars would never do this. Why would he? He's a good guy, Emma. Besides, I barely knew the man. There's no motive."

"Maybe you're right. But don't you think it's sort of weird that he's the only other person on that list who lives on the lake with a boat that you know besides Birch?"

Joey shook his head. "No, not really."

"Just ask Mr. James where he was Saturday morning. That should clear the question," Merek said.

"I really don't ..." Joey started to say something before Emma interrupted.

"And ask him about his boat. He'll understand. He's a cop," Emma said. "Besides, he might be able to help us."

"Can't hurt. I'll call Sammy and Cook and tell them to talk to him," Joey said.

Edith came into the room.

"Hey, there, beautiful," Joey said.

She shook a finger at him, then at Emma. Emma put both hands in the air as if surrendering. "He makes me do it, Edith. Besides, if I didn't bring it to him, he'd just get it delivered," she said.

"Don't you be making excuses for him," she said. "And you, Mr. Reed. Don't you think you can sweet talk me into anything. I've heard it all," Edith said.

"Now, Edith, Edith. You know I'm telling the truth. You are beautiful. I'd never try to pull the wool over your eyes. Ain't no way."

She harrumphed, talking under her breath.

"What was that?" Joey asked, grinning.

"I said you of all people should know that you need to take better care of yourself. Cops are smart people."

"That we are," Joey said.

"Whatever you say," Edith said. "I have to go, but I'll be back. You'd better clean up that mess," she said, looking at the wrappers. She left the room.

Merek stood from leaning against the wall and said, "We need to scram, Miss H. I must go to run errands."

"Oh, that's right. When's Natalie get here?" Emma asked.

"In the morning," Merek said.

"Whoa. Hold up." Joey raised a hand in the air. "Natalie, the married lady from Kentucky with a couple kids?"

"*Tak*. She is no longer married. She is divorced. So, yes, that Natalie. She is singing at The Worthington Inn tomorrow evening, and Emma and I are going to attend."

"I'm looking forward to it," Emma said. "I can't wait to meet this dark-haired lady who's won Merek's heart."

"Merek, what's going on with you, dude? Talk to me," Joey said.

Merek smiled. "I think she is *the one*."

"Right," Emma said, rolling her eyes.

"No. I have not felt like this before." He put a hand on his chest.

"Right," Emma said again. "Merek's in love—again. That's never happened. Well, I must say, it's never happened with a dark-haired woman that I know of. Speaking of women, have you talked to Fantasy?" she asked Joey.

He nodded. "Yeah. I talked to her late last night. She's in an extended-stay hotel and talking about moving out of town. She asked me for your number. She said she wanted to call and thank you personally for being nice to her after lying to you and Merek. Is it okay to give it to her?"

Emma shrugged. "I guess. I sort of felt sorry for her when we were on the boat. I mean, she saved Birch's ass from drowning and he was probably going to try and kill her out there."

"And I likely saved her ass, but she doesn't believe me. You know it's too bad she's got a screw loose. She really does have a good heart," Joey said.

"Oh, dear, no," Emma said. "Don't even think about it."

Joey shook his head. "Ain't no way. Besides, I've met someone myself. She could be *the one*."

"Who, Mr. Joey?" Merek asked.

"A cute nurse, right?" Emma said.

Joey shook his head "No, she's a doctor."

"Well, well. Look at you, Mr. I-want-to-settle-down-too," Emma said. "Do tell, Lieutenant Reed."

"Yes, Mr. Joey," Merek said. "Tell us more about this doctor."

"Not yet. I don't want to jinx anything."

***

"I love the wine selection here," Mary said to Samuel, as they strolled the aisle, looking at all the bottles. "They have different tasting events here and a mozzarella cheese making class. Charles took the class and brought some to the house several times. It's delicious."

"The meat and fish counters are extraordinary, too," Samuel said. "This place is wonderful. How'd you find it? What's it called again? Weiland's Market? And it's family-owned, you say?"

"Yes. Locals refer to it as Weiland's. Emma and Charles told me about it. They always shopped here. I make a point to drop by whenever I visit. I imagine Emma still shops here. Her place is only a few blocks away," Mary said.

"It reminds me of a grocer in England. I love it not only because of the food but because it's also small and family-owned. I get overwhelmed in those big groceries. They should offer maps upon entering," Samuel said.

They were interrupted by someone calling her name.

"Ms. Mary." The voice was familiar. She turned to see Merek standing behind her. She looked up at him.

"Merek Polanski. So nice to see you," Mary said. "How have you been?"

"I am fine, thank you. How are you?" Merek made a mental reminder not to say anything about Charles or his father if she mentioned it. He glanced at the man with his arm wrapped through Mary's. "*Cześć*. I mean, hello," he said to Samuel.

"Hello," Samuel said.

"Merek, this is Samuel. He lived with Charles and me years ago. He was Charles's tutor. Samuel, this is Merek Polanski, Emma's ... office helper. He's originally from Poland. He and Emma helped discover Devereux's underhandedness and put him behind bars."

Samuel extended his hand and Merek gave it a strong shake. "So wonderful to meet you. Mary told me about you and Emma Haines and the fine work you do training insurance fraud investigators. But I had no idea you helped her incarcerate Devereux."

Merek's ears burned as he nodded. *Office helper?* he thought. "Thank you. Yes, we did assist. But it was mostly the police. Mr. Joey."

Mary made a small gasp. "I read about him again in the paper this morning. Brexton Birch and Joey's ex-girlfriend? And Mrs. Birch hired someone to kill him? What a fiasco."

"*Tak*. It is as Mr. Joey says, 'a big mess.'"

"Emma and I had dinner at my place earlier this week. I'm sure she must have mentioned it to you."

"Yes. She said she had a nice time," Merek said. Emma did mention it. She told him about faking a phone call to get away from Mary.

Mary eyed Merek's full cart. "It looks like you're stocking up or having a party," she said.

"I am having a visitor from New York City. A beautiful lady singer. She is coming for the weekend. I pick her up at the airport in the morning."

"Well, you don't say. That's wonderful. You know, that gives me an idea. I think I'll throw a dinner party while Samuel's here. Would you like that?" She turned to Samuel.

"A dinner party sounds wonderful. But don't go out of your way just for me," he said.

"Nonsense. I should've thought of it sooner. That settles it. I'm throwing a huge dinner party. I'll let you and Emma know as soon as I set a date. And you can bring your New York lady friend," Mary said. "Will Emma be bringing Stratton? She didn't say a word about him the other night."

"I do not know, Ms. Mary," Merek said.

"Well, I know he's still in Europe on his book tour," Mary said. "Odd that she isn't there with him. I'm sure everything is fine between them. Besides, what business is it of mine? She must have more pressing business here than being with him, I suppose."

Merek shrugged. He wanted to get away from Mary Wellington. "I would love to stay and talk with you, but I have an appointment. Please excuse me. I look forward to your invitation. I will tell Emma. I gotta scram," he said and nodded.

"I understand. Preparations before your friend arrives. Nice to meet you, and have a lovely weekend," Samuel said.

"Yes. Good seeing you, Merek," Mary said.

Merek hurriedly pushed his cart toward the registers.

"Nice boy, but so odd. And all those tattoos and earrings. Makes him look rough. And I have a difficult time understanding him through that accent of his." Mary gave a little shudder.

"He seems like a perfectly fine gentleman. I understood him perfectly," Samuel said.

"He's always scramming. That strikes me as rude."

"Oh, Mary. Not everyone has your manners and grace. Shall we continue our shopping?"

***

Merek walked out of Weiland's Market and loaded his groceries into the saddle bags on his Harley. He threw his leg over the seat, put on his gloves and helmet, started the engine, and rode out of the parking lot onto Indianola.

After he put the groceries away, he cleaned the condo, even though it was spotless from the visit by the cleaning company the day before. When he finished, he sat on the couch and flipped through TV channels. He turned it off. He was bored and restless. He didn't want to call Natalie again. Too much, too soon. But he had to do something.

He flipped through his phone and found the address again for George's Marina. He'd already talked to the owner about Joey's accident, but he wanted to go back and talk to other people who worked there.

***

James Mars looked up from the front desk of the showroom as a man dressed in leathers rolled into the lot on a loud motorcycle. The man shut off the engine and dismounted. He stood and looked around at the boats in the boatyard as he slowly took off his helmet and placed his gloves inside it.

The tall man had tattoos on his neck and the backs of his hands. He wore small ear, nose, and eyebrow rings. He strode into the showroom, holding his helmet. He looked around the showroom, which displayed four huge motorboats, waiting for a dock to call home.

"Hello, there. How may I help you today, sir?" James Mars asked. "Can I interest you in one of those fine beauties or something outside on our lot?"

Merek shook his head. "They are beautiful, but I am not here to buy a boat."

James felt his skin prickle. "Then how may I help you?" he asked again, standing a bit taller and wondering why George never took his advice about buying a firearm to keep under the counter.

"My name is Merek Polanski. I am a friend of Lieutenant Joey Reed. He was run over by a speedboat while he was kayaking last weekend."

James nodded. "Oh, my. Yes, how terrible. I read about it in the paper and saw it on the news." He paused and put on his best smile. "Are you a police officer?" Merek shook his head. "No, just a friend. I am trying to help him."

"I see. I assume you're here inquiring about the boat that may have been involved?" James said.

Merek nodded. "*Tak*. I am looking to know of anyone with a white boat with a windshield and a dark canopy with spots on top. This is the boat that ran over Mr.

Joey."

James rubbed his chin. "Spots on top?"

"Yes, on top of the cover over the driver."

"Oh, you mean the Bimini."

"*Tak*. I mean yes."

James's ears grew warm. He hadn't heard about this from Cook or Sammy. "We've not had anyone rent a boat or bring one in like that," he said. "Hmmm, I'll tell you what. I'll put a note on the employee bulletin board for everyone to see, telling them to contact you and the police. Do you have a phone number?"

"That would be good," Merek said and handed him a business card.

James looked at the card. H.I.T. He remembered. Emma Haines. The woman who was with Joey Reed the day of the accident and the woman he'd met at the station.

"You're a fine friend looking into who may have done this. You see, I'm a retired detective myself."

"And what is your name, sir?" Merek asked.

"My name is James Mars. I work here part-time. You can rest assured that I'll let my friends at the station know if we see any kind of boat like you've described." He smiled at Merek. "Are you sure I can't interest you in a boat? From what I see, I can tell you're a man of speed and adventure." He looked past Merek to his motorcycle. "That's a fine-looking Harley you've got there, Mr. Polanski."

"Thank you, Mr. Mars," Merek said. "*Nie dziękuję*. No, sir. I do not wish to buy a boat. Thank you for your time." He walked outside and sat on his bike. The engine roared to life as he glanced around the lot. Several cars, including a black Volvo covered in bird droppings, sat at the end of the building.

***

After Emma and Merek visited Joey that morning, she ran errands and decided that it was a nice day to kayak and do more investigating. She walked Millie, ate lunch, loaded her boat and drove to Twin Lakes. She studied the map she'd printed, folded it, and put it in her pocket. She got out of her truck and unloaded *Arlene*. She put on her life jacket, placed her paddle and red metal can of water in the boat, and locked her truck.

She picked up the bow handle on the nose of *Arlene* and pulled it into the grass and down along the side of the boat ramp. When the nose of the kayak rested in the water, she zipped her life jacket, stepped into the kayak, sat down, and scooted off the land using her body momentum and her paddle.

A great blue heron squawked as she paddled right around the first bend. Six mallard ducks bobbed in an inlet, and cardinals sang to one another from different locations. A catbird whined from a tree and a house wren chattered. *Birds are so loud for their size,* Emma thought.

She adjusted her floppy sun hat and pulled down the sleeves of her SPF swim shirt.

She continued to paddle through the culvert under Route 745 and past the few houses that lined the left bank. It was the same path she and Joey had paddled. She looked ahead as two more blue herons flapped their wings lazily through the sky. Cormorants sat in a tree, wings open, drying themselves. A kingfisher gave its high-pitched, choppy call as it flew to a dead branch jutting out over the water. A small fish flopped in its beak seconds before the bird swallowed it.

Gulls floated on the open water ahead and several swooped up and down over the reservoir—white birds in a clear blue sky. An osprey dived into the water and shot up without a catch. It circled higher and out of sight. It could've been the same bird that she and Joey had seen.

She paddled onto the open water where she had told Joey not to go. She sat straight, braced her feet against the foot pegs, and began paddling to the far side of the reservoir. She loved to watch the bow as the kayak parted the water like a knife. On the far side of the lake, she turned left along the bank, where several houses began appearing behind low water walls, docks, and landscaped yards.

Twenty minutes later, she sat in her boat in front of a small cove covered by trees. It was dark and cool and reminded her of the mango groves in Florida she'd kayaked. She paddled into the inlet.

James Mars's dock jutted out into the water in the middle of the tree canopy. A boat port sat on one side of the dock. Her heart sank. There was no boat. She studied the area and the back of the brick ranch house. A bay window looked out over a wide yard that sloped down to the water. The yard was full of trees and flowers. She saw no one.

A silver grill and iron porch furniture sat facing an outdoor fireplace on a rock patio. A rock walkway and steps led from the patio to the dock. A paved drive along the edge of the woods curved from the front of the house down to the water, where it fanned out into a small boat ramp. She paddled closer to the property.

Chickadees, mourning doves, cardinals, woodpeckers, goldfinches, and nuthatches flitted among several different types of bird feeders. Blue jays, sparrows, and starlings also flew from the feeders into the woods and trees above her and back to the feeders. Several robins hopped around, looking for that next big worm. A Carolina wren and a catbird called from the woods. An orange-chested Baltimore oriole hopped from branch to branch before it flew away.

Emma watched the show and wondered how often the feeders had to be filled to keep all these hungry birds happy. She sat in her kayak taking in the surroundings. *Maybe Mr. and Mrs. Mars were out for a boat ride,* she thought.

After several moments, she turned and paddled out of the inlet following the shore as it curved left. She'd kayak downstream in the shade along the shoreline until she was directly across from the water on the other side of the reservoir that went into Twin Lakes. There, she'd paddle straight across the open water.

James Mars steered his boat into his inlet seconds after Emma paddled into the neighboring cove.

***

Joey sat in a chair with his leg propped on a stool. He watched the cars come and go in the parking garage. He'd counted more Hondas today than any other make of car. His survey was interrupted.

"Hey, there."

Joey smiled. "Just the person I was dreaming of. Come on in."

Dr. Amy Fields rolled her eyes. "Right," she said as she walked over to him.

"You've got to let me out of here. I'm going crazy,"

Joey begged.

"Well, I'll see what I can do about that, but I can't do much about your going crazy. I think anyone who wants to be a cop is already a little crazy." She smiled.

"And anyone who wants to be a doctor isn't?" Joey asked.

She laughed. "Good point."

"I love your laugh. And if I'm going crazy, it's only because I'm in here and not out dancing with you after we eat at the finest restaurant in town," Joey said.

"Lieutenant Reed. Are you flirting with me? Again?"

"Absolutely. Remember, you promised me dinner."

"I remember." She flipped through his chart and jotted notes. "I'm putting you in a walking boot and cutting you free today. What do you think of them apples?"

"Seriously?" He shouted. "I think those are some mighty sweet apples. I'm counting cars in the parking garage to keep sane. I can't take much more. I should've been out of here sooner, you know."

"Whoa. Slow down. Who's the doctor here? I wanted to make sure you didn't have any internal damages. You had a serious blow to your head. That's why your room was dark for a few days and I kept you as long as I did. But everything looks fine. You're good to go if you're careful."

"And here I thought it was mood lighting," he said.

She grinned. He continued, "Is that the *only* reason why you kept me in here?" He turned on the "Joey Reed smile."

She returned the smile, blushed, and stood. "Look, I know that Edith has been wheeling you around outside in the garden and making you use crutches and the scooter. I'll have her come in here with the boot and wheel you to the curb. You'll need a ride home, so call someone. I want you out of here."

"This is fantastic. You're a real gem. By the way, what's your favorite gem?"

"Gem? You mean as in diamonds?"

"Yes. You're my diamond girl," Joey said.

"Isn't that a song?" she asked.

"It is. How do you know that?"

"I listen to the oldies station," she said.

"Ouch. That hurts," Joey said, putting his hand on his heart.

She patted him on the shoulder. "Cheer up, Mr. Reed. You'll be walkin' on sunshine in no time."

"And don't it feel good?" Joey sang, as he pumped his hand in the air. His cell rang. He glanced at the phone and picked it up.

"Emma, I have great news. You need to swing back by here again because I need a ride home."

***

James and Lucy ate their supper in the dining area of the Alzheimer's center. They chatted about their day. James told her about the tattooed man that came to the marina, but he didn't tell her who or why.

"All over his body?" Lucy asked.

"Well, I can't say for certain. He had on a leather jacket and pants. But he had tattoos on his neck and the back of his hands. I suspect he had many more. It was appalling."

Lucy giggled. "Remember when Jimmy wanted to get a tattoo? Remember what you told him?"

"Only two kinds of people have tattoos, military and

hoodlums."

"That was it. But he got one anyway," she said.

James looked shocked. "I don't think he did. I would've known."

Lucy patted his arm. "Wives don't tell their husbands everything."

"You mean ..." he trailed off.

She put her finger to her lips. "Shhhhh ... I don't want him to hear us talking about this if he comes in." She winked and continued eating her mashed potatoes.

James pushed his lima beans around with his fork. *Jimmy had a tattoo? How did I not know this?* he thought. He looked at Lucy. *I wonder how many other things she never told me.* But he didn't care as he looked into the sparkling blue eyes of the woman he loved, living inside a woman who didn't even know him. He reached out and took the hand that was in her lap and began to cry.

"Oh, Lucy, I miss you so much," he babbled, kissing her hand. "I miss you so much."

"Come, come now. I'm sure she misses you, too," Lucy said, patting the top of his hand. "This Lucy person must have been a wonderful woman from what you've told me about her. Now, get a hold of yourself, dear sir. Eat your supper."

He nodded and sat up. She gave him a smile and patted his arm. "Isn't the roast beef marvelous? I just love coming here to eat."

"Yes. I'm glad you like it here. It is a nice place."

"It is. And people here are so friendly. I just love their outfits. Some of the ladies wear shirts and pants with little pink and blue doggies and kitties on them. Reminds me of when my son was a baby and we bought him a blue stuffed dog. He loved that dog."

"Gimper," James said, through a sad smile. Gimper could be in Arizona with his grandchildren or they could've thrown him in the trash. He started to cry again.

"Oh, dear. I'm sorry you're upset. What's wrong?" Lucy asked with deep concern in her voice.

He dropped his head. "I miss my family so much. It makes me so sad and angry."

"I'm sorry," Lucy said and patted his hand again. "I'm so sorry. But life goes on. It's just the way it is."

***

After dinner, James walked to his car and climbed behind the wheel. "How long was this going to go on? Why? Why? Why?" he yelled. He beat the steering wheel with his fists. After several moments, he took a deep breath and calmed down. He took his cell out of his pocket and tapped a contact.

"Hey, James. How are you?"

"Not so good, Sammy. I was just wondering if you wanted to grab a beer. I just had dinner with Lucy, and it was a rough one. I need to talk to someone."

There was a long pause. "I'd love to, James, but we've got folks over for dinner. You're more than welcome to come by and join us."

James frowned. "No, no, I wouldn't think of imposing. We can do it another time."

"Are you sure? It's no problem at all. Come on over. The more, the merrier. Are you okay?"

"Yeah, I'm okay. I'm fine. And no. I can't come over. I wouldn't be good company. But I'm fine," James said, disappointed.

"Look, maybe we can grab a beer tomorrow night,"

Sammy said. "Hey, I'm sure sorry about Lucy. I really am. She's a wonderful woman."

"Thank you, Sammy. She is. Or was. It's just that some visits are better than others. Anyway, how are things down at the station?"

"Good," Sammy said.

"You hear any more on the Reed accident?"

"No. Nothing. We'll probably never know who did it. I'm sorry I had to ask you where you were last Saturday, but you living on the lake with a boat and all. And Joey asked me to."

"I'd have done the same thing. Sign of a good cop. I do live on the lake, but like I said, I was at the marina early and no one knew because I was alone in the warehouse."

"That's fine, James. It's not an issue at all," Sammy said.

"Listen, I'll help you guys any way that I can. You know that. But I'll need to be kept in the loop, just so I can help. Reed's a fellow cop and was a friend of Jimmy's," James said.

"Right, I understand," Sammy said.

James heard talking and laughing in the background.

"Hey, James, I need to run. The crowd's getting rambunctious over this Monopoly game we've got going on here. It's my turn, and I'm winning."

"Well, you'd better go then."

"Yeah. I seldom win, so it's exciting. I'll talk to you later, James. Goodbye."

"Bye," James said and ended the call. He sat in his car staring out the window. Tears slid down his cheeks.

Saturday, July 26

"FLIGHT 94 FROM New York City arriving at Gate 12," the voice came over the speaker. Merek dodged people as he hurried through the John Glenn Columbus International Airport. He finally stood in the rear of a crowd at Gate 12, holding a bouquet of flowers. He watched as people filed off the plane. *Would she look the same? Would I look the same to her? Maybe this was crazy,* he thought.

About twenty people walked through the gate into the airport. Some hugged. A few scurried by with rolling luggage or a briefcase, talking on their cellphones. Some looked happy. Some stressed. Some tired. Some blank as a robot.

Finally, an extremely tall, slender woman with shoulder-length, ebony hair and bright red lipstick strolled through the door as if she were walking down a runway. She carried a black guitar case. Long silver earrings dangled from her ears. She pulled a leather carryon bag behind her.

He took a few steps and waved to her. She nodded, making her way toward him until she was standing in front of him, looking down into his eyes. She was several inches taller than him.

"Merek Polanski. Fancy meeting you here," she said with a wide grin. She kissed him on the cheek.

"New York Natalie. You are more beautiful than I remember," he said, catching a whiff of her familiar perfume. "These are for you." He handed her the bouquet. She looked at it for a long moment before she took it. "I adore wildflowers. How did you know?"

He shrugged. "I bought them because they are beautiful and they remind me of you."

"I'll bet you say that to all the girls. How are you?"

"I am good." They stood, looking at each other with wide smiles on their faces. "You play guitar when you sing?"

"Yes, I took lessons. I figured it would be easier to carry than a piano." They laughed then fell into an awkward silence.

"I will fix us brunch at my home," he blurted.

"That sounds fantastic. Flying always makes me hungry. I think it's the stress."

"I will take your bag," he said.

They walked through the airport. She held the flowers and carried the guitar and he pulled her bag. She slipped an arm around his.

***

"How in the world did you learn to cook like this? The different dishes ... and that cold soup. This meal was amazing." Natalie said. She wiped her mouth on a silk napkin Charles had sent Merek for Christmas last year.

"My mother. We cooked together when I was a boy and when I was in Poland recently. She makes the best

Chłodnik. That is the cold soup. I was not sure if you would like it."

"It was amazing. There are so many flavors here with the kielbasa and pierogis and the soup. Don't tell me you made the kielbasa and pierogis, too. If you do, I may have to marry you."

He smiled and said, "If it had not been for you, I do not know if I would have gone back to Poland. What you said to me in Kentucky made me go back home. I stayed for nearly two years."

"And what you said in Kentucky inspired me to go back to school, which likely led me to a divorce. Which was good. It had been a long time coming. Isn't it funny how one thing is connected to another by a few passing words? It fascinates me," she said.

"That is true. I look back and think that if Emma had not walked into the computer store looking for a laptop, I may not be here with you. I, too, am fascinated."

She looked around. "Your place is amazing."

"Thank you. This, too, is because of Emma Haines walking into the computer store."

"Emma Haines. I can't wait to meet her."

"*Tak.* You will like her. She is a beautiful, smart woman, like you."

"So you've told me. And she sounds like a firecracker."

He nodded. "She is. You will meet her tonight when you sing. I cannot wait to hear your beautiful voice again."

"You're too kind. I love singing. And Sally is following in my footsteps, it appears. She bought a guitar and is taking lessons."

"Ahhhh. Yes. Your daughter." He looked away from

her. A silence fell in the room.

"Tell me about your trip to Poland. How was your visit back home?"

Merek told her about his trip and how his family had convinced him that he belonged back in America.

"And you don't want to move back to Poland?" she asked.

He shook his head. "No. I belong here. That I now know. Before I went back, I thought I might move back home to stay. But no. My life ... it is here."

She smiled. "Yes. *We're* here now."

He stood and walked around the table. He held out his hand. She took it. She stood and he pulled her close. She wrapped her arms around his neck, and they kissed.

"I made *all* the food myself. Now, you will have to marry me," he whispered.

"I'll think about it," she said.

He kissed her again.

"Okay. I'll marry you."

***

Emma was at her kitchen table reading *The Columbus Dispatch* and sipping coffee. Millie trotted into the kitchen, her toenails clicking on the tile floor.

"Hey there, baby girl. What are you into today?"

Millie yawned, did a long doggie-down stretch, and wagged her white-tipped tail.

"Just gonna hang out and take it easy with me? Mama's got no plans until this evening, when Uncle Merek and Uncle Joey and I are going to The Worthington Inn to hear Uncle Merek's *latest* girlfriend sing. You know how Uncle Merek is. But don't worry. I'll be back in time to take you on your evening walk. How's that?"

Millie's basset brown eyes watched Emma. The dog wagged her tail faster. She turned, walked to her food bowl, and stuck her nose into it. She licked it a few times before she took a long drink.

"You know, you have such a rough life. You live better than many people in this world. Do you know that?"

The dog stood, staring at Emma and wagging her tail.

"Licking your bowl clean, huh?" Emma said as she got down on the floor to pet Millie. The dog was soon on her back, her paws in the air. Emma scratched Millie's pink-spotted belly. "You got it so bad," she said, kissing the top of Millie's left front foot. "Just look at them big feeters. Just look at them." Emma placed her hand beneath one of Millie's front paws. It covered her palm.

Suddenly, Millie flipped onto her feet and barked. She turned and ran through the condo and up the stairs. Emma followed. "You wanna play?" she said as she chased the dog up the stairs.

Millie ran circles around the bedroom before she jumped on the bed, panting, wagging her tail, and barking.

"You know you're not supposed to be on the bed, silly girl. What are you doing?"

Millie barked, jumped off the bed, and ran down the stairway into the kitchen. Emma followed.

"You are so silly," Emma said as the dog walked in circles and started to dig in her bed. She walked in a few more circles and lay down.

"I think you wore both of us out." Her cell rang. She walked over to the marble counter and picked it up. She checked the screen, looked puzzled, and hit the accept call icon.

"Hi, Rhonda. How are you?" Emma asked.

"Oh, hello, Miss Emma. I'm fine. Just fine. I was wondering how you were getting along. I haven't talked to you in so long, and you were on my mind. I just wanted to call and say hello. That's all. Yes, we're still at Stratton's. I just came in from watering all the plants outside, and it's so hot. I set up the sprinkler to water the garden after I watered the flowers. Is it hot up there? You could fry an egg on the sidewalk down here. Yes, you sure could. The hills are steaming. And this humidity is so hard on my hair. It just droops down and I have to put more pins in it and use more hairspray. Well, just the other day, I had to go to the Dollar Store and buy more hairspray. I don't go through hairspray like this in the winter. No, my hair is much better in the winter. This is just awful. Just awful what this humidity does to my hair. And then I think Maggie was so hot, just so hot. She ran around the yard with her tongue hanging out and saw me setting the sprinkler up in the garden and just jumped into the water to play in the sprinkler.

"Can you believe that dog? She jumped right in there and started biting at the water and hopping around and barking. It was the funniest thing. She just played and played in that sprinkler for a long time. I think she'd have stayed in there all day. She misses Stratton, I'm sure, but she was having such a good time in that water. Yes, that's for sure."

Emma smiled as she pictured Stratton's secretary spraying and pinning the white ice cream swirl on the top of her head above her bony face, complete with drawn-on eyebrows, bright orange eyeshadow and orange lipstick. She wondered if Rhonda had an entire wardrobe of orange polyester clothes. Every time she'd seen Rhonda, she had on an orange outfit of some kind. The woman even wore orange shoes and orange plastic jewelry.

Rhonda rambled on. "Have you talked to Stratton?"

When she paused to take a breath, Emma jumped in and said, "I'm fine, Rhonda. It's good to hear from you. No, I haven't talked to him the past few ..." She couldn't remember the last time they had talked. "I'm sure he's busy."

"Oh, well. Yes, I'm sure he is busy, on his book tour and all. But he should make the time to call you, I would think. After all, if he hadn't been kidnapped when you two were kayaking in Kentucky, he wouldn't have a best-selling book in the first place, now would he? Just never mind. It's not my business."

Emma frowned as Rhonda went on. She didn't want to think about Stratton right now. Or the fact that she had started to call him several times but stopped. It could be because they hadn't had a great deal to say to each other the last time they talked. He went on about all the restaurants he was going to and how many books he'd sold. When he mentioned her coming back to Europe, she put him off—again. She asked him when he was coming home and he put her off. He loved Europe. She leaned down and scratched Millie. *Why are relationships so difficult?* she thought.

"Oh, now, what timing," Rhonda said. "Oh, dear, I'm sorry. I have to go. Someone's at the door. Now, who on earth could that be? Anyway, I wanted to tell you that I saw that wretched woman who was Earl Calhoon's girlfriend—that Martha woman. I saw her in the grocery the other day, and she had a child with her. Did they ever catch him after he got out? You know, Stratton is worried sick over that. He's afraid that man may come after you again. That's one of the reasons he was so upset when you left Europe and went home. He is so worried about that."

"I know. We've had this talk a million times. I doubt Calhoon will bother coming around here. I don't think he's that stupid. He's probably out of the country by now."

"Well, I don't know, but I have to go now. I'm so sorry. I wanted to talk longer. They keep pounding on the door. I'll call you later when we can talk more. Bye."

When I can listen more, Emma thought.

"Bye," Emma said and tapped the icon to end the call.

Her cell rang again. She grabbed it, half expecting it to be Stratton. She didn't recognize the number. She was in no mood for another telemarketing call. She hit accept, ready to hear the recorded message about her loan being preapproved or a new credit card but heard something else instead.

"Hello? Is this Emma Haines?"

"Who's calling?" Emma said. The voice sounded familiar.

"This is Fae Vernon. Did I call at a bad time?"

Emma squinted. "Fae Vernon?"

There was a pause before the woman said, "Fantasy."

"Oh. Yes, hello. I'm sorry. Yes, Fantasy. How are you?"

"The first thing you should know is, I'm not going by the name Fantasy anymore. Those days are over. My name is Fae, and that's what I'd like to be called. Secondly, I was wondering if I could buy you dinner sometime. Just to thank you for, you know. That's all."

Emma didn't reply.

"I mean, it's okay if you don't want to. I just thought, well, if you want to. I'm not doing it to get close to Joey or Merek or anything like that, either. I'm done with them. In fact, I'm planning on moving away as soon as all this is over. Just wanted to thank you. That's all," Fae said.

Emma paused. "Sure, what were you thinking?"

"How about tonight? I know it's Saturday, and it's late notice. But if you don't have any plans… Or tomorrow for lunch or something."

"I can't tonight. But I could meet you somewhere for lunch tomorrow. How about the Wildflower Café?"

"Sure. As long as Merek won't be there. I know he used to go there all the time. He used to take me there. I like that place, but I don't go in there because he might be there."

"Oh, that's true. Sorry, I forgot. I'll make sure he won't be there. How's that?"

"That sounds good. Want to meet there at 11:30?" Fae asked.

"Okay. See you then. Bye."

"Bye."

"This day's turning out to be pretty interesting," Emma said to Millie. The dog yawned, stuck her nose under her paws, and closed her eyes.

***

Emma and Joey peeked out from behind the blind of her front bay window. A blue Hyundai sedan pulled in front of the condo. Merek and a tall, dark-haired woman unfolded from the car.

Emma and Joey smiled at each other. "The one," they whispered in unison. The front bell rang, and Emma opened the door. "Hello, hello. Please, come in," Emma said as she stepped aside.

"Hello, Miss H., thank you." Merek and Natalie entered.

Merek wore black jeans and a white T-shirt under a black linen jacket, and black loafers without socks. He looked like a different man and he carried a guitar case. "Miss H. Mr. Joey. This is New York Natalie."

"I'm so pleased to meet you, Emma. Merek's told me how you met and all about your company," Natalie said, shaking Emma's hand, then Joey's. Natalie wore a loose red silk shirt, tailored jeans, and red wedge sandals. The red of her fingernails matched her toenails and bright red lipstick. Her makeup and hair were perfect. A pair of dangling silver earrings caught the light. She was striking.

"It's nice to meet you, too. Merek told me about meeting you in Kentucky and that you'd reconnected. It's all so exciting," Emma said. "I can't wait to hear you sing. It's all he's talked about."

"I'm looking forward to hearing you sing, too," Joey said.

"Thank you. I'm so sorry to hear about your accident," Natalie said.

Joey nodded. "It'll all be okay. I've got the private care of my doctor." He turned to Merek. "You carrying a weapon in that case, Merek? I know you don't play a guitar."

"I just didn't want to leave it in the car. He offered to carry it for me," Natalie said.

"You can set it on the couch. Let's go in the kitchen. I made a few snacks and we have champagne to celebrate," Emma said.

"That is so kind of you, Miss H.," Merek said, placing the guitar gently on the couch.

"Yes, it's so thoughtful," Natalie agreed.

They walked through the small living room, passing the two white love seats facing a small coffee table that sat in front of a fireplace. When they were in the kitchen, Merek called for Millie. The basset came trotting into the room, wagging her tail. She went to Merek and he squatted to pet her. "Uncle Merek hasn't seen you in a while," he said. "Have you been a good girl? I'll bet you have." Millie licked his face.

"What a gorgeous basset hound," Natalie said. "Look at that sweet face and those long ears." Merek stood, and Millie went over to sniff Natalie. "May I pet her?" she asked Emma.

"You'd be breaking the law if you didn't," Emma said, laughing.

Natalie leaned down and talked to the dog while she scratched and petted her. Millie wagged her tail and licked Natalie's hand. "Such a sweet girl," Natalie crooned. Soon, Millie was on her back, legs in the air. Natalie gave her a few rubs on her tummy before she stood and looked around the kitchen. "What a cozy place," she said.

"Thank you," Emma said as she took the wrapping off a tray of snacks sitting beside four champagne flutes and a bottle of Veuve Clicquot Rosé that was chilling on ice in a silver bucket. "If you'd like to wash your hands after petting Millie, go right ahead." Emma motioned toward the large marble sink on the other side of the kitchen.

"Thanks," Natalie said. She and Merek headed toward the sink. Emma and Joey smiled at each other as Natalie and Merek leaned into one another while they washed and dried their hands.

Emma handed the bottle of champagne to Merek. "I'll let you do the uncorking. I'm afraid I'll shoot someone's eye out. Go outside on the patio if you need to," Emma said.

"No problem, Miss H." Merek said and carefully removed the cork. He filled the glasses and set the bottle back in the ice bucket. He handed everyone a glass and raised his. "To New York Natalie. The most beautiful woman with the most beautiful voice in all the world," he said.

Natalie blushed. "To new friends," Natalie said, raising her glass.

"And to new relationships," Emma said. They clinked their glasses and took a sip.

"Hear, hear," Joey said.

Millie wagged her tail as if she were part of the celebration before she walked over and curled in her bed in a corner. Everyone sat around the kitchen island and talked.

***

Two hours later, Merek, Emma, and Joey sat at a round table in the The Worthington Inn bar area. Natalie sat on a stool behind a microphone strumming her guitar. She began to sing *A Case of You,* by Joni Mitchell and made a great deal of eye contact with Merek. He grinned from ear-to-ear, his piercings sparkling in the light.

Emma leaned over and squeezed his arm. "You're right about her singing *and* her beauty."

"I am in love, Miss H.," he whispered into her ear. "She is *the one*."

***

After the evening at The Worthington Inn, Merek and Natalie went back to his place and Emma drove Joey to his house. "It's great that you're home," Emma said as they sat in his front room.

"It's great to *be home*. I'll be back to work Monday. I was going crazy in that hospital."

"I can imagine. Well, no, I really can't. As many times as I've been in a hospital, I've been the visitor."

"Good for you," Joey said. "I've been in and out a few times. Worst was when I got nicked by a bullet from some jerk I was chasing through an alley."

"I've been shot at. And it's weird. If that wouldn't have happened, I'd never have started H.I.T. or met Merek or Stratton. Anyway, I'm glad you're home. I thought Edith was going to throw me out of there if I brought you any more McDonald's."

Joey waved a hand and laughed. "Yeah, I've not eaten that much junk in years. Luckily, I didn't gain an ounce."

"You probably burned it off chasing your new doctor friend. How's that going?"

He shrugged. "Okay. That's all I'm saying right now. She's busier than I am, which could be a problem. I asked her to go this evening, but she had rounds at the hospital. But I'm sure we can work in a few dates." He winked.

"Well, she's a different type of woman for you. Speaking of different types of women, what do you think of Natalie?" she said.

"I've dated professional-types before. But she's *totally* different than any of the women he's dated. She's beautiful, yeah, got that model look. And she's a few inches taller than him. And she's *not* blonde. She's definitely got that New York City look. Money," he said.

"Classy all the way. But divorced with two young kids. She can sing, no doubt about that. Merek swears she's *the one*," Emma said.

"You think she is?" he asked.

She shrugged. "I don't know. But the way he looked at her was pretty amazing. It was fun to watch him watch her. But this one's got a lot more baggage than his other flames. And she lives in Manhattan."

"There's planes. And people move, you know?" he said.

"Don't even say that," Emma said, holding up a hand. "I've almost lost him twice. I really don't want to think about losing him again."

"Emma, you don't own the man just because he works with you. He's got a life, you know. Third time's a charm. He'll be gone."

"I could never replace him. He's too, too … perfect."

"Yeah, he is a good guy. And no one else would put up with you the way he does. Maybe they'll just fly back and forth for a while, see how it goes.

"By the way, he told me he talked to James Mars at the marina. He works there part-time. Probably a good job for him since he's a boater and retired," he said.

"I couldn't believe all the birds in his yard when I kayaked over to his house. It looked like that Alfred Hitchcock movie. I like birds, but this place was over the top. There were at least two dozen feeders in that backyard. They were mostly full, so someone had filled them recently. Birds were flying everywhere. Reminded me of Crab Bank Seabird Sanctuary off the coast of Charleston and that rookery in Florida, where I've kayaked.

"Is there anywhere you haven't been kayaking?" Joey asked.

She laughed and stood. "Plenty of places. Hey, I'm really tired. I need to head out. I want to take Millie for a quick walk, and I've got a lunch date with someone. You'll never guess who it is."

"Who?" Joey asked.

"Fae Vernon."

He rolled his eyes. "Have a good time. And tell her she's welcome for me saving her butt, even though she doesn't believe it."

Sunday

Natalie walked out of Merek's guest room into the kitchen. "Whatever you're making smells wonderful."

"Good. I am making breakfast for you. I baked fresh *chleb zwykły*."

"What's that?"

"Polish bread," he said.

"You're kidding. Merek, you didn't have to do this for me. All these fine meals and the get together at Emma's. Now this? You're both very kind."

"This is not special. I bake *chleb* often."

"Are you serious?" she asked.

He nodded as he poured eggs from a bowl into a skillet. "I was waiting to hear the shower go off to begin the eggs. It is not good to overcook food."

"I never imagined you were such a great cook, too. And look at that table setting."

He grinned. "I am great at many things. A bang whiz."

She smiled "I'll bet you are. May I get myself a cup of coffee?"

"Please sit and I will get it for you. Black?" he said.

"What a great guess. How did you know?"

He shrugged. "I am not a guesser. I know." He tapped the side of his head.

He poured coffee into a mug and set it in front of her. He kissed her on the cheek. "You sang so beautiful last evening. I am so glad you are here." He walked back to the stove.

"Thank you." She paused. "I'm glad I'm here, too. But I do miss Sally and Kenny. I didn't exactly tell them everything about this weekend. I just told them I'd landed a gig in Ohio, and they were happy for me. I also knew they had the weekend at their dad's when I thought up this little trip."

Merek chuckled. "You thought about this for some time?" he asked.

"Since the first time you called."

The kitchen was silent except for the spatula in the skillet as Merek scrambled the eggs. His back was to Natalie as a smile grew across his face.

"Anyway, I had a wonderful time and appreciate you letting me stay here."

"I would not let you stay anywhere else," he said. "You are welcome here anytime."

He scraped the eggs onto a plate and pulled warm bacon from the oven and placed it on another plate. He set it all on the table. He poured himself coffee and sat down. He turned to her. "Do you pray before you eat?"

She gave him a puzzled look. "No. But if you do, go ahead. It won't bother me."

"No. I do not. My mother does. I just did not want you to feel uncomfortable if you do."

"You're an incredibly thoughtful man, Merek Polanski."

"My mother raised us as a Catholic family in Poland.

Please, eat before it gets cold."

She scooped eggs onto her plate and added a strip of bacon. Merek placed a piece of warm bread on the side of her plate.

"There is butter and strawberry jam in the containers," he said, pointing to small crystal, covered bowls.

"Thank you." She spread butter onto the bread with a dab of jam. "How did you know I wasn't a vegetarian?" she asked.

"You ate meatballs last night at Emma's," he said.

"Not only thoughtful, but observant. I like that."

He grinned, then turned serious. "When does your plane leave?"

She glanced at her watch. "In six hours. I have plenty of time."

"Good. I will show you the sights of Clintonville. We will go to the Columbus Park of Roses first. It is beautiful. Everything is blooming. The roses, they will wilt when they see your beauty."

"You're such a charmer. Are we riding your motorcycle?"

He pulled his cell from his pocket and checked the weather. "If you would like a ride, the weather is good."

"I would love to take a ride. I've never been on a motorcycle, except my brother's dirt bike when I was a kid."

They ate and shared more about themselves. Afterward, they cleared the table. He kissed her.

"You're a great kisser," she said.

"You are so beautiful," he said, tracing one of her cheeks with his fingers. "Let's go see the roses."

She cocked her head. "You know, you're quite the gentleman. Most men would've tried to get me in bed the first thing."

He kissed her neck. "I want to make love to you more than anything. But I want our relationship to be more than sex," he said.

"Wow." She paused and gave him a shocked look. "Okay, then. Let's go take a ride and see those roses," she said.

"Here, you wear my spare leather jacket and gloves, even though they will be very large for you."

She put on the jacket. It hung on her everywhere. They laughed and walked out the door, her arm wrapped around his.

***

Emma saw Fae, who sat at a corner table in the Wildflower Café. She walked over and sat down across from her.

"I'm glad you suggested this place. I've always liked it here, but …" Fae trailed off.

"You have nothing to worry about," Emma said. She'd texted Merek to steer clear of the restaurant since she knew he might want to bring Natalie there for breakfast or lunch.

"Thanks," Fae said.

"It's nice of you to buy me lunch, but it's not necessary," Emma said.

"I just wanted to say thanks. And I'm sorry I lied to you and Merek. I wanted to tell you about that video so bad."

"Obviously, not that bad," Emma said.

Fae looked down at the table, "I did. But I couldn't get Brexton in trouble."

Emma looked at the top of Fae's head. She sighed. "It doesn't really matter at this point. But don't lie about something important that could ruin other people's lives. Especially to a cop. They'll find out sooner or later. Okay? You could've saved everyone a lot of trouble," she said, sternly. She paused. "Anyway, what's going on with all that?"

Fae nodded like a scolded child. She raised her head. "Brexton is likely dealing with his divorce. I haven't talked to him," Fae said with a sad frown.

"No big surprise there," Emma said, giving Fae a look.

She shrugged. "Hey, look. I don't care that I split them up. That marriage was dead for a long time. And I can honestly say, I didn't mind being the other woman. It was sort of exciting, and I'd never had that kind of money or that nice of a place to live. Being a pole dancer and a waitress doesn't pay all that much. And I was in love with him."

"Was?" Emma asked.

"I never want to see him again. All I want to do is get away from here and start a new life."

"Where to?" Emma asked.

"I'm thinking of somewhere south. I'm tired of the winters here. Maybe Charleston or someplace like that. I still have money in my checking account from Brexton, and I intend to use every cent of it."

A waitress came, took their orders, and left.

"Just for the record, Fantasy—sorry—I mean Fae. I seriously doubted it was you who ran over Joey. But it was hard not to suspect you and Brexton."

"Really? What do you mean?"

Emma stared at her. "I wasn't convinced it was you

because of what you just told me, and I doubted Brexton Birch would want to do something like that, being who he is. But we may have been wrong there. Joey and I believe he planned to leave you in Lake Erie. Did you have any idea that he might be going to try to kill you when you were on the yacht?"

Fae shook her head. "No. I don't think he would hurt anyone. But he did say he should've gotten rid of me sooner. And he called me a worthless slut. That hurt. I thought he really loved me. Anyway, love is definitely blind. I still can't believe he can't swim. What a jerk."

Emma said, "You also knew where and when Joey and I were kayaking that day because he accidentally texted you. And you had 'Boat Ride' written on your calendar on Saturday, the nineteenth. That certainly made me wonder. And the calendar was gone when Merek was at your place."

"Yeah. At first, I thought the text was from Brexton, but I didn't understand why he'd be sending it to *my* phone. Then I noticed it was from Joey's number and I got the second text from him that said he didn't mean to send the first one. I deleted them both. I really didn't give it any thought and I sure didn't mention it to Brexton. But I threw the calendar away because of what was on it, in case the cops came," Fae said. "Did you see anything on Brexton's video that shows who ran over Joey?"

"Nope. Too far away," Emma lied. She wasn't about to tell this woman anything.

"That's too bad. I was hoping it would help," Fae said.

"Me too," Emma said.

Fae looked at Emma for a long time before she smiled and asked, "You from around here?"

Emma shook her head. "Chillicothe. About an hour south."

"I think I've driven through there. Pretty area. Lots of hills." The waitress set their drinks in front of them and left.

"You planning on living in Clintonville forever?" Fae asked.

"Sure. Why not? I love it here," Emma said.

"Just wondered. Some people just want to move, I guess. I know that Merek nearly moved to Colorado for some Polish woman. I was surprised he came back from Poland. Anyway ... You date anyone?"

Emma eyed her. She wasn't used to giving information to strangers. Only getting it. "Yes," Emma said.

"Oh, that's right. I heard about him. He wrote a book or something?"

"Or something," Emma said.

The waitress put a Southwest chicken salad in front of each of them. "Anything else I can get for you ladies?" the waitress asked.

"Nothing for me, thanks," Emma said.

"Me, neither. Thank you," Fae said.

"Okay then," the waitress said and left the table.

They ate in silence for several minutes. Emma's cell vibrated in her purse. She got it out and read the screen. Charles.

"Excuse me, I need to take this call," she said as she stood. Fae nodded and continued eating. Emma walked outside into the parking lot.

"Hey, Charles. What's up?"

"Emma, I'm exuberant. I've found a house. I'm arriving Thursday to view it and I want to reconnect with everyone. Would it be possible for you to host a dinner at your place on Saturday? Would you do that for me?"

"Wow! You really are moving home. I'm so happy. Sure, I can get the gang together. Want me to pick you up at the airport or anything?" she asked.

"No, thank you. I'll rent a car and stay at Mother's or a hotel."

"You're not bringing your dad?" she asked.

"No, he's staying here. He trusts me to buy the best home for our comfort. Traveling tires him and he has the boys to look after."

"That's good that he has the dogs. It is a long trip. Should I invite Mary?"

"Yes, of course. I'll call her immediately. I hope she's not in one of her moods. Dinner at your place on Saturday then?"

"You got it. Six o'clock. I can't wait. I'll just have Weiland's cook everything and I'll pick it up."

"Fantastic! I'm scheduled to see the house at two on Thursday. It's only two point one miles from your place. I'll text you when I've finished and stop by. We can discuss the dinner details then."

"I can't wait to see you," she said.

"Likewise. Goodbye for now."

"Bye." Emma put the phone back in her purse, walked into the restaurant and sat down.

"You sure look happy. Good news?" Fae asked.

"The best," Emma said.

"Must be nice. I could use some good news," Fae said.

Emma didn't say anything. "When are you planning on moving?"

Fae shrugged. "I'm going to drive down south next week and check some places out I've looked at online. I'll live in an apartment, then maybe buy a place. Who knows? I may even get my GED and go to college. Merek always told me to do that."

"Good for you. I think that's a great plan."

"Yeah, I figure, why not? I'm still young and have my looks. I'm sure I'll meet someone down there. Maybe I'll get married and have a family. That's what I want. You ever want kids?"

"No. I wouldn't be a good mother. I'm too selfish."

"You ever been married?"

"No. Too confining." Emma said as she glanced toward the wall clock. She'd had enough of Fae Vernon. "Look, I appreciate lunch, but I need to get going." She pulled her wallet from her purse.

Fae held up a hand in a stop position. "Lunch is on me. An apology for being so mean to you and I wasn't being nosy, just trying to make small talk. I'm not very good at it," Fae looked sadly sincere.

Emma took a deep breath. "That's okay." She stood and pushed her chair in. "Thanks for lunch, Fae. I wish you all the best."

***

"Samuel is *there*?" Charles asked again.

"Yes. He's visiting. We're having a lovely time," Mary answered as she sipped a martini.

"Mother, are you drinking?"

She ignored his question. "I'm throwing a dinner party this Saturday night in his honor. I'm inviting everyone. Emma, Stratton, that Merek Polish helper of hers, and my golfing partners. It's a shame you can't make it."

She glanced down at copy of *Senior Women's Golf* magazine lying on her desk. Her picture was on the cover. She smiled at the magazine and took another large sip of her drink.

"But Mother, that's why I'm calling. I'm coming home to look at a house and Emma is planning to have everyone for dinner Saturday evening—at her condo."

"A house? You're moving back here?" Mary yelled into the phone.

"Yes, I am. I'm retiring, and I'm going to work for a Labrador rescue," Charles said.

"Why didn't I know about this? You didn't tell me first. Is the house near here?"

"I'm telling you now. I'm moving back to Clintonville. That's my home."

"Oh, I see. I'm sure Emma's known about this. I imagine everyone knows about this but me, your own mother," Mary said with a sneer. "You know I have adjoining land that you could build on. A house to suit you perfectly. Far enough away from me, but closer. I wouldn't think you'd want to move back to Clintonville with all those horrible memories of Simon swirling around there."

"I'm completely over that and all that happened. I attended exceptional counseling here in Switzerland, and I'm quite ready to come home. I'll be fine," Charles said.

"Counseling? My son in counseling? I cannot believe that!" She took another drink. "That aside, I'm glad you're coming back. It's where you belong. But I do worry about you living alone and being lonely."

"I'm not at all lonely," Charles said, watching his father walk toward his chair in the great room. He wasn't about to tell her about him over the phone. No, that would definitely be one for a face-to-face discussion. Or a face-to-face brawl as Charles imagined.

"Oh, yes. The boys," she said.

"Sadly, I only have two now. I had to put Sam down several days ago."

Mary took another drink. "I didn't know. Why didn't you call me? You never share anything about your life with me, you know."

"Because I didn't want to bother you about it," he said.

"I would not have been bothered. I'm sure you called Emma," she spat.

"Never mind, Mother. What shall we do about Saturday evening?"

"Just tell Emma to have her little party here. We can merge the two. She can invite anyone she likes. I want this to be a festive occasion."

"Are you celebrating something?" Charles asked.

"Yes. My son has finally come to his senses and is moving back here. And I'll have another surprise, I'm sure."

"I certainly hope you don't plan to propose a toast using those exact words. What's the other surprise?" Charles asked. His left pinky began to twitch as it always did when he became nervous or something unfortunate was about to happen. It was a trait he inherited from his father's side of the family, or so his father told him.

"I can't tell you yet."

"All right, then. What were you thinking of serving Saturday?" Charles asked.

"I'll let John handle it," Mary said.

"Perhaps you should invite John and his wife as guests and cater the meal. Emma was picking up food from Weiland's."

"Funny. Samuel and I were just there. We were taking a drive and ran into Merek in the wine section."

"You were at Weiland's? Why were you in Clintonville?"

"No reason, really. Just out taking a drive after lunch."

"I see. Consider giving John the evening off and catering the affair," Charles said.

"I'll think about it," she took another drink. "I'll handle everything from here. I'll call Emma and let her know the party will be here and that she'd better bring that handsome Stratton Reeves with her," she slurred.

"Oh, Mother."

"Toodles," she said and ended the call.

***

"I just called Emma and Mother and informed them about the house. Mother's shocked, but happy," Charles said to his father. "My realtor tells me this house is stupendous and, of course, large enough where we'll both be comfortable while retaining our privacy. It won't be a problem. It never has been. We've discussed this numerous times. Stop worrying. I enjoy your company. And we'll be close to Emma. I'm looking forward to kayaking with her again. Maybe you can even join us. I'll buy a tandem. I think you'd enjoy it." Charles said as he stood in the doorway between the kitchen and great room. His father, Charles Wellington II, sat in his recliner, looking out the window at the Swiss Alps.

"Your mother's going to flip when she finds out about us. You're a good son, in spite of my not being there while you were growing up. I regret not trying to get in touch sooner. I should've been . . ." He turned and looked at his son. "Are you sure I'm not a burden?"

"You are not. You probably even saved my life, storming into it the way that you did. Otherwise, I would've had more time to stew over all my misfortunes. You've kept me company these past years. You're not getting rid of me, I'm afraid. And Mother will simply have to deal with it," Charles said.

"Son, I know I've said this before, but I'm truly sorry about Simon. I wish I'd have known him. From everything you tell me, he was a kind, caring man. And what he did is beyond bravery."

Charles nodded and went back into the kitchen.

Charles's mother had given his father his walking papers when Charles was a baby. But his father had returned, unannounced, and demanded that Mary tell Charles the truth that he didn't leave his son and that she had kicked him out.

At first, Charles was shocked that his father had come back into their lives. He feared he was simply looking for a handout from his golf-celebrity mother. But he wasn't. He just wanted his son to know the truth. Charles and his father became close without Mary's knowing. Charles even paid for an apartment and supported him in Clintonville. *"We certainly wouldn't want to upset her. She simply doesn't need to know,"* Charles had told his father. And they agreed. They'd been getting along splendidly and living together ever since.

"Don't put too much powder in the chili," Charles's father yelled toward the kitchen.

"I wouldn't dream of it," Charles yelled back as he stirred a large pot of chili in the crock pot. He took a taste and added more chili powder. He took another taste. Satisfied, he replaced the lid and walked back into the great room.

"Father, I'd appreciate it if you could stir . . ." He stopped and a smiled. His dad was snoozing peacefully in his leather recliner. Cecil and Cleo lay at his feet. He walked over to the chair and draped a small throw blanket over him. "Sweet dreams, Father" Charles whispered.

Monday

"I LIKE IT. We can do this," Calvin Nelson said, leaning back in the conference room chair.

"Good," Emma said, looking away. She disliked Monday morning meetings. On top of that, Calvin wasn't wearing an undershirt and the sight of his bare stomach peeking through the gaps between the buttons made her stomach turn.

"You've done it again," he said. "Now, let's go have lunch and celebrate." He smiled at her as he rocked in the chair.

"That's it? That's all you've got to say? How did I know this would lead to yet another lunch invite? You should take Merek to lunch. These are his ideas. I'm just presenting them."

Calvin lifted his right hand and studied his fingernails. "I've had one to many lunches with him. I don't like him. He may come up with good stuff for this company, but I don't like him one bit."

"This is why I made him my partner. He does great work," Emma said, gesturing toward the computer before crossing her arms and leaning back in her chair. "We're a team. And we deliver 'good stuff,' as you call it.

It's not just 'good stuff.' It's valuable research. H.I.T. saves you a ton of money and you know it, Calvin."

The room fell silent.

Calvin gave her an evil grin. He smirked and picked his teeth with a fingernail. "Tell you what. You come back to Matrix and work for me, and you won't need a partner. I'll pay you more money than you could ever dream of."

"No way. It's much more than money. You don't get it. At all," she said.

"Ole man Matrix would love to have you back here. In fact, he's mentioned it to me several times. He's not getting any younger. Me and you, we should be running this company. We'd make millions. We'd be rich," Calvin said.

"You're already rich. At least that's what you tell me. And how do you define rich?" Emma went on before he could answer. "Big houses? Fancy cars? Lots of money? Beautiful women on your arm? Merek and I do just fine."

"You do fine because of me," he said. "Matrix pays you a lot of money—because of me." He pointed to himself. "And you know *that*, little Miss Vendor."

"And because of Mr. Matrix," she said. They held a stare.

"Why do you make this so damn difficult?" he asked, leaning forward and smacking the table.

"I don't," she said. She stood, placed both palms on the table and leaned over him. "You need to cool your jets, Mr. Nelson."

He grabbed one of her hands and held it, hard. "Emma, think about it. You and me. Nelson and Haines Insurance. Or Haines and Nelson. I'd even let you have your name first. But it should be the Nelson Insurance Company."

Emma pulled her hand away. "There's laws against this kind of *stuff*, Calvin. It's called harassment and *you* know it. But I've tolerated it since I first met you—laughed it off, tried to ignore it. 'Oh, it's just the way he is,' I've always said. But it's getting old. Really old. I should report—"

He leaned back and interrupted her with a loud chuckle. "Go ahead. Report me to HR or even to your police buddies. You have no proof. My word against yours. And I've done nothing but try to be nice to you. And you've taken my money for years without a peep. So who would they believe?"

She jerked the plug from her laptop and shoved the computer into her bag. "You know, it's none of your business, but I'm thinking of retiring," she said, not looking at him.

Calvin snickered. "You're not even fifty and you're going to retire?"

"I've had enough of all this," she said. "Enough of you and presentations and working and everything. And I really don't need to work."

"Oh, that's right. How is your rich old man, Stratton Reeves?" Calvin said, sarcastically.

"None of your damn business, Mr. Nelson," she snarled.

"I'm offering you the chance of a lifetime, and you're treating me like this. You've always treated me poorly, Emma. Never any respect. And I've done nothing but pay you big money and try to be nice to you. Come on now. Be nice." He leaned over and rubbed the back of his fingers against her arm.

She slapped his hand and slung her bag over her shoulder. "Save it, Calvin. And don't ever touch me again.

You pay me for this presentation, and we're done. I'm done. H.I.T.'s done. With you and Matrix and everything. You know? Maybe I will report you," she said, heading toward the door. She stopped and looked down at the top of his hair-plugged head.

"And I don't mean to HR or to Joey or the police. To Stratton and Merek. I'm done with you, Calvin Nelson!"

She slammed the door behind her and stomped down the hallway.

Calvin frowned as he propped his dirty, size-thirteen shoes on the desk. He clasped his pudgy hands over his belly, which peeked through the gaps in his shirt. "I need to do something about her. I certainly do," he said aloud.

***

Emma pulled into her office drive. She hit the brakes so hard the tires squealed and she rocked in the driver's seat. She got out of the truck, grabbed her computer bag, slammed the door, and huffed up the steps into her office. Merek sat with his feet propped on the small conference table. He was studying his cellphone screen. He looked up when she burst through the doorway and slammed the door behind her.

"Hey, Miss H. What is the trouble? Mr. Calvin did not like the presentation?"

"OH, NO! Just the opposite. He *loved* it," she said, throwing her bag onto the love seat in the waiting area.

"Then what is the problem?"

She dropped down hard on the couch and put her head in her hands, rubbing her face and temples.

Merek got up from the chair and sat beside her. He

put his arm around her shoulder and pulled her into him.

"Merek, I just don't know. I can't live like this anymore. I don't know what to do. I think I just blew both of our incomes and our future with Matrix. I lost it. I can't take Calvin Nelson anymore. I totally blew up at him. Told him that H.I.T. was through with him."

Merek patted her back. "Miss H., I am glad. It is time you stopped taking his *gówno*."

She sniffed and looked at him. "You're not upset? I always tell you to keep your cool with him, and now I go and do what I tell you not to."

"Miss H., I keep my cool, but I let Mr. Calvin know that he is an asshole without saying it. I told him he must stop his movements toward you."

"Yeah? When? Because he must've forgotten. He's such a creep. I don't care how much he pays us anymore. We're done with Matrix. I mean it." She got off the couch and paced the waiting area.

Merek stood, fists at his side. "Did he do something to you? If he did, I will go—".

She interrupted, shaking her head and holding up a hand. "No, no. He just grabbed my hand and proposed. The normal and usual crap from that, that . . . whatever you call him."

"*Świnia*. Pig."

"Yeah, that. Anyway, I'm done with him, Merek. We're done with him. Seriously."

Merek shrugged. "That is fine with me. We will find other companies to work with."

She stopped. "You know something, Merek Polanski?"

"You could not live without me?"

They high-fived each other. "You got that right.

Let's get to work on some sales materials. I've never had to make any, but I'm sure we can get a testimonial from Mr. Matrix. I'll call him later, once I calm down," she said.

"This is good, Miss H. Are you going to tell this to Mr. Stratton?"

She shook her head. "No, it's not his problem. Its mine. We just won't take Calvin's *gówno* anymore."

Merek stood. "*Zgadzam się*. I will design a sales brochure for us," he said.

"Sounds good. How can I help?" she asked.

"I will review online and then we will make a, a ..." He stopped and looked at the ceiling, searching for a word as he sometimes did. "Prototype together," he said.

"Okay. I'll look at some, too. Maybe this is what we both need. New clients and a new beginning."

"*Tak*," he said.

"*Tak*," she repeated as her cell rang. She took it out of her purse and looked at the screen.

Emma put the cellphone to her ear. "Hey, Joey. How's your first day back?" Merek went into his office and closed the door.

Merek and Emma each had their own office. They were actually small bedrooms before the building was zoned commercial. Emma had rented the space before they met, and they both liked it. There were four suites, and H.I.T. was on the lower half of the former brick apartment complex on High Street, near the Whetstone Library. Emma's condo was nearby, and he only had a short drive from his glass tower condo along the Olentangy River.

"It's good to be back. I'm a little clunky in this boot, but I'm getting around. I won't be chasing anyone for a while, though," he said.

"I'm glad," she said.

"Listen, I just talked to Sammy and Cook. It's probably nothing, but I wanted to run it by you."

"Okay. What is it?"

"They said that James Mars has been *super* interested in my case."

"You said they're buddies and he's a retired cop and you were at his house once," she said.

"Yeah. A lot of cops retire and miss it. But I don't really know this guy at all. And he hasn't talked to me. I think he would."

"You want me to go talk to him? I know where he lives," she said.

"No. Just wanted to bounce it off of you."

"Are you suspecting him?" she asked.

"No. No. Like I said, I don't even know the man. Why would he want to run over me in a boat? I was only at his place once with Jimmy for a beer and that was years ago. Anyway, he's probably just interested because he's a bored, retired cop. Gives him something to do. Not sure why he doesn't talk to me about it, though," Joey said.

"I'll go talk to him to if you want me to," Emma said.

"No. Leave it to Cook and Sammy. I just wanted you to know. They'll handle it."

"Sure, okay" she said.

"So how'd your big presentation go to that guy you work with at Matrix this morning? Nelson? That his name?"

"Yeah. Calvin Nelson. Not so good. I blew up at him. I think I've told you about all his moves he's made on me for the past million years, right?"

Joey chuckled. "What happened?"

Emma told him everything.

"This has been going on forever, now, Emma. You want me or one of my guys to have a talk with him?"

"No. It's not his fault I put up with him for all those years, but I'm telling you, Joey. Merek and I are through with Calvin Nelson and his bullshit. We're putting together a sales plan to pitch to other insurance companies. We're through with Matrix."

"Sounds like a plan. Look, I gotta run."

"Okay. Bye."

The call ended. Emma noticed that Merek's office door was closed. He was probably working on the sales brochure. She smiled and went in her office to look at a few online. She was nervous, but excited.

***

Merek sat at his desk, pulled his cell from his pocket, and hit the icon in his *Favorites* that read "New York Natalie." He sat down at his computer, facing one of the three windows.

"Hi, Merek," she answered cheerfully.

"Hello, my sweet," he said. "Do you have time to talk?"

"Of course. I always have time for you," Natalie said. "You at work?"

"*Tak*. I mean yes."

"Merek, it's fine when you talk in Polish. In fact, I think it's sexy. But I want you to teach me Polish so I'll understand."

"Sexy?" he asked.

She laughed. "Yes. And your accent is a real turn-on, too. Since the first time you spoke to me in Kentucky."

He smiled. "What are you doing today, New York

Natalie?"

"I'll be there in a minute, sweetie," Natalie yelled away from the phone. "Merek, can you hold on just a sec? Sally needs me."

"*Tak*, Yes," he said. He began to search for sales brochures on his computer. He reviewed several before Natalie finally came back to the phone.

"I'm sorry about that. Hey, I'll call you back later this evening when the kids are in bed, okay? It's just not a good time right now."

"Yes. I understand," he said.

"I'm sorry. I'll call you around ... nine. Will that work?"

"Yes. I will count the seconds," he said.

"Bye, sweetie."

"*Pożegnanie*."

He ended the call and laid his phone on the desk. He leaned back in the chair and looked around at the pictures on his walls. Brutus Buckeye and many pictures of the The Ohio State Buckeye's football and basketball teams covered one wall. Family pictures from his last visit to Poland covered another. Miscellaneous prints of various Polish artists were on the other walls. He studied a picture of himself and his family taken in his parents' kitchen by a visiting cousin when he was there.

Marriage. Wife. Children. Family. The words swirled in his head as he could hear Natalie saying, "I'll always have time for you," then, "It's just not a good time right now."

It was becoming clear to him that she may seldom have time for him. Not now. And likely, not ever. No matter how much she wanted to.

But he was so attracted to her. She was different

from other women he'd met, and she already had children. If they married, he'd have an instant family. *A family*. He closed his eyes and recalled the conversation he had with his mother in the kitchen while he watched her cook. His parents knew little English, and he spoke only Polish while he was there. He was wondering if he should return to Clintonville.

"Your life is in America. You must return," his mother had said.

He paused for a long moment before he nodded and said, "Yes, I know. But you are here. You and Father come to America and live with me."

She shook her head. "Our lives are here. You will marry and have your own family soon. There."

He had gazed out the window and sipped tea wondering if he would ever marry and have a family. He wanted to settle down, but it just had not happened. But then again, blonde strippers who danced at the *Messenger Club* weren't his idea of a wife. He'd had too much fun for too long. He needed to stop going there and expand his horizons. He needed to talk to New York Natalie, the woman he thought of every day since he'd seen her.

"I will, yes. But you need to come to America so I can take care of you," he had said.

His mother looked at him. Flour covered her cheek. He wanted to grab her and take her with him. "You are the one who left Poland and started a new life, Merek. We do not belong in America. You do. Go back. Your brothers will take care of us."

And that was that. He made the choice all those years ago when he saw an ad for The Ohio State University in a magazine at the grocery where he worked while getting his computer science degree from the *Uniwersytet*

Warszawski. An American co-worker, who was a student at The Ohio State University majoring in Polish studies, had shown it to him and helped Merek speak and read English. Merek helped him to learn Polish. They taught each other about their native countries.

Merek had dreamed of attending The Ohio State University and becoming a Buckeye, playing an instrument in The Best Damn Band in the Land, also known as TBDBITL. So he went to America, where he'd met Emma while working at a computer store in Clintonville, and everything changed in an instant. *Funny how life turns on a dime, just as it had once again*, he thought. Merek was proud that Emma did what she did, but this would impact both their lives. Tremendously. Good or bad.

He would be thirty soon and knew that if he didn't marry and start a family, it would never happen. He glanced out the window. "Are you really the one, New York Natalie? Or am I just in a dream? But you came to see me. You did that." He sat looking out the window for several minutes. "Yes. That is it. I will go to see you," he said and began googling flights to New York City.

***

Emma tapped on Merek's door. He walked out of his office into the waiting area.

"I keep thinking about Joey's call." She told him about their conversation. "Anyway, did you find any brochures you like?"

He nodded. "*Tak*. Nice ones. Do you want to get lunch? I can print them, and we can talk about them."

"You know, I think I'm going to go kayak around

James Mars's house again. We can talk about brochures later."

"But Mr. Joey told you to leave it to the other officers," Merek said.

"I know. And I will. Take the rest of the day and do whatever you need to do. I'm going to go home and walk Millie, then load my boat and go back out to O'Shaughnessy."

"Got it, Miss H. And I need to tell you that I do not think I will be at your party for Mr. Charles on Saturday." She'd invited him earlier that morning.

"Why not?" she asked.

"I am going to New York," he said with a huge smile.

"Oh, okay. That's fine. How long will you be there?" He shrugged. "I do not know. I am surprising her."

"Wait. She doesn't know you're coming?" she asked. He shook his head. "I am leaving today and will be there soon. I will go to her house and surprise her. I do not know what day I will return."

"You think surprising her is the right thing to do? I mean, it's pretty early in your relationship, don't you think? Maybe you should ask her if it's okay. She's got kids, Merek, and an ex-husband around. And you just saw her yesterday."

"It will be fun to surprise her," he said.

Emma looked at him for a long moment. "Do what you need to do."

"Thank you, Miss H." He went back into his office, shrugged into his leather biker jacket and walked back out into the front office.

"Okay. We'll talk marketing when you get back," she said.

"*Tak*. I will let you know when I will return," Merek said and left the office.

Emma watched him get on his Harley and ride away. Her cell rang and she went into her office. She looked at the screen and sighed. "Hello, Mary. How are you?"

"I'm fine, Emma. I was calling to invite you and Stratton to my dinner party I'm having here Saturday. Charles said that he spoke to you and you were going to call me to come to your apartment Saturday for a dinner party. Let's just have it here. It's much more suited for parties."

"That's fine if you'd like, Mary. You do have more room at your place." *It's not an apartment, it's a condo,* Emma thought.

"Yes, *much* more room. Oh, and by the way, I ran into your office help at Weiland's. Did he tell you?"

"My business partner," Emma said.

"Whatever he is. I told him to invite his friend from New York and come to the party."

"Merek told you about Natalie?"

"Oh, is that her name? He didn't mention her name. I'm dying to meet her," Mary swooned. "I haven't thrown a good party in a long time. And I want everyone to meet Samuel."

"Samuel?" Emma asked.

"Yes. He was Charles's tutor when he was in school. He lived here with us for several years."

"Oh, yes, I remember Charles telling me about him," Emma said. *Uh-oh. Poor Samuel,* she thought.

"Will Stratton be coming with you?" *She just never stops,* Emma thought.

"I doubt it. He's still in Europe. I don't think he'll be back this weekend."

"Oh, really?" Mary said, a sarcastic lilt in her voice. There was a long pause.

"Look, Mary, I have to go. What time and what should I bring Saturday?" Emma asked, already knowing the answer to the last part of her question.

"Be here by seven, and don't bring a thing. It's certainly disappointing that Stratton won't be joining you. It's been a long time since I've seen him."

Emma ignored her. "I'll be there. I may bring Joey Reed. But Merek probably can't make it, either. He'll be out of town."

"I see. That's certainly disappointing. My parties are always so wonderful. It's too bad he'll miss it. And yes, please bring Detective Reed."

"Lieutenant. He got a promotion two years ago when he busted Deverux," Emma said, unable to contain herself.

"I see." She paused. "Well, Good for him. I'll see you Saturday around seven. Toodles," Mary said.

***

Emma pulled into the Twin Lakes parking lot, unloaded her boat and gear, and slid out onto the lake. The sky was clouding with the promise of a much-needed shower to cool down the hot day. But she figured she had time to paddle to Mars's place and back based on the forecast. Emma didn't mind getting rained on, but she wouldn't paddle in lightning.

She paddled past the scene of Joey's accident toward Mars's house. Even though Joey advised against it, what harm could her talking to him really do?

She made her way into the open water. Gulls dipped

and soared above her, and a white egret stood along the far bank. A half-hour later, she sat under the trees beside Mars's dock. There was no sign of a boat or James Mars.

The feeders were empty and birds sat around, expectantly. She paddled over to the boat ramp. As she got out of her boat and pulled it onto the ramp, a bird sitting on a branch above her pooped on *Arlene's* bow. She frowned and shook her head. "Don't poop in my seat," she said toward the bird.

The thick, green grass had recently been mowed. Due to the size of the lot, she imagined James Mars on a riding mower. The flower beds needed weeding.

She walked up the ramp to the patio, up the driveway to the crest of the yard and made her way to the front porch. She rang the doorbell. A weedy bed of Black-eyed Susans swayed in the summer breeze under windows with closed blinds. The sky was growing darker. Now she wished she'd driven instead of kayaked.

No one answered after several rings of the bell. She knocked. After sensing no movement inside the house, she made her way back around the house, down the sloping yard. She sat in the kayak and scooted backward off the boat ramp into the water. She used her paddle to splash water on the bow in an attempt to remove the bird poop, with no luck.

Back at her Tacoma, she loaded *Arlene* and pulled her phone from her drybag. Two messages. Stratton.

She leaned against the back of the pickup and hit the return call icon. He answered on the third ring.

"Emma, are you all right?" he asked, sounding concerned.

"Yes. I'm fine. Why?"

"I've left several messages and texts, and you haven't

answered me. I was worried. I was just about to call Merek."

"You worry too much," she said.

"Is something wrong?" he asked.

"No," she lied. "How are you?"

"The book tour is splendid. But I've convinced my agent that enough is enough. I'm coming home in two weeks. Could you please pick me up at the airport?"

"Sure."

"Emma, is something wrong?"

"As a matter of fact, yes. Rhonda called me. She told me you're still super-worried about Earl Calhoon coming after me."

"It does concern me. We've discussed this. She didn't see him, did she?"

"No, but she saw his old girlfriend, Martha. And she had a kid with her."

"A child? Hers?"

"Beats me. Who knows? I heard she was pregnant when they got busted," Emma said.

Silence. "I see." More silence.

"So, it could be his kid. I don't know and I don't care. He's long gone. He wouldn't risk it. Even he's not that stupid," she said.

"Emma—"

"Let's drop it," she snapped. "I've got other things to think about."

"Like what?" he asked.

"Like they can wait until you get home. It's nothing."

Silence.

"It's good to talk to you, sweetie. I miss you," he said.

She sighed and looked at the ground. "I miss you,

too." A long moment passed. "Okay, so let me tell about what's going on here," she said. They discussed Joey's accident.

"I'm so glad he's recovering. I hope the boater is caught soon," Stratton said.

"Yeah. About all we have to go on now is that the Bimini is spotted on top. Like polka dots or something. But a boater can get rid of one of those things and buy a new one, from what I've read. But I've never seen a spotted one online. Maybe it was custom-made," she said.

"Hmmm. That is interesting."

Emma told him about Charles returning and Mary's party.

"Unfortunately, I can't be home by Saturday. I'm sorry I'll miss all the fun. But I'm glad Charles is coming to look at a house. I assume he's bringing his father."

"Not this time. But when he does, they're going to break that news to Mary together. Charles wants me to be there. I'm guessing he'll need a referee."

They laughed.

"Maybe I'll take Joey to the party. I'll ask him," she said.

"What about Merek?" Stratton asked.

Emma proceeded to fill him in on Merek and Natalie. "I don't look for him to be back by Saturday."

"Seems there's lots of catching up to do. I've got several more bookstores, a few libraries, and a university talk first. I'll call you when I have my flight information."

"Okay."

"I'll talk to you soon. Bye-bye," he said.

"Bye," she said. She ended the call. Thunder rolled through the sky and it started to rain.

***

"We'll be landing at Gate 5 in LaGuardia in about ten minutes. The weather is hot and humid with a chance of showers. Thank you for flying with us today. It's been a pleasure. Flight attendants, please prepare the cabin for arrival," the pilot's voice announced.

Merek closed the tray into the seat in front of him and fastened his seat belt. He handed the steward an empty cup and a peanut bag.

As he walked through the airport, tapping his Uber app. A driver arrived and took him to the hotel. Merek checked in, went to his room, took a quick shower, and ordered room service. After he ate, he checked Natalie's address. He glanced at the clock. It was five thirty. He tapped the Uber app again and made his way to the lobby and climbed in another Uber driver's car.

The driver pulled in front of a Manhattan brownstone, and Merek got out. He looked up at the door. He suddenly felt awkward and thought of ordering a ride back to the hotel. He and Natalie had just been together a few hours ago. Maybe Emma was right. But he was here, and he had come to see her. This would prove how he felt about her. He climbed the steps and rang the bell. Seconds later, she opened the door.

"Merek. What a surprise!" she said with a huge smile. "What are you doing here? It's so good to see you. Come on in and meet Sally and Kenny," she said, hugging him.

Merek hugged her back, feeling relieved. "Are you sure this is okay?" he said. "I just wanted to see you."

She looked at him and held his face between her hands and kissed him. "Oh, Merek."

"Mom, who's *that?*" A young girl stood in the hallway behind Natalie. She looked frightened.

"Sally, honey, come meet Merek. This is my friend I was telling you and Kenny about."

The girl stood fast, staring at him.

"It is a pleasure to meet you," Merek said.

"He talks funny," Sally said.

"It's not *funny*. He's from Poland. Remember, I told you. You have many friends at school from different countries with accents. You have an accent to them, too. We've discussed this. Remember?"

Sally continued to stare. "Nice to meet you, too," she mumbled in a whisper.

"Mom, where's my baseball?" a boy yelled from inside. A few seconds later, he appeared behind Sally and looked at Merek. "Wow!" the boy said.

"I am Merek. And you must be Kenny," Merek said.

"Yeah, that's me."

"Very nice to meet you, Kenny."

"Wow! Look at all those tattoos and earrings," Kenny said. "Can I touch them?"

"Kenny, that's not a nice thing to say to anyone," Natalie scolded.

Merek bent down. "Sure. It is fine," he said.

Sally stood without moving while Kenny rushed forward and examined Merek closely, touching his eyebrow rings and earrings, and rubbing his fingers on the tattoos on Merek's neck and hands. "Cooooool," Kenny said. "Why do you have all those earrings and tattoos? Are you in a circus?" Kenny asked.

"No, I just like them," Merek said, standing.

Kenny looked up at Merek. "I like them, too. And your coat. And you're so big. Way cool."

"Thank you," Merek said.

"Kids, why don't you run along while Merek and I talk in the kitchen?"

Kenny turned to Natalie. "Mom, I can't find my baseball, and Dad's going to take us to the game this weekend."

"It's in your room on the bookshelf. I put it there after I found it in your bed," she said.

"Oh, okay." Kenny turned back to Merek. "Wow! So cooooool."

Sally stood in the same spot, staring at Merek. "Sally, please go help your brother find his baseball," Natalie said. Sally slowly turned, following her brother.

"I am sorry this is a shock for them," Merek said.

"It's New York City. They're used to many types of people. Just not in our house, I guess. Or coming to see their mother." She smiled and fiddled with her diamond necklace. "It's wonderful to see you. Let me take your coat. I'll fix us something to drink," she said.

"Thank you," Merek said, and handed her his biker jacket, and followed her down the hallway into a brightly lit kitchen. He climbed onto a stool at the counter. "I am sorry I did not call. But I wanted to surprise you."

She hung Merek's jacket in a small closet and came into the kitchen. "Let's be serious. You wanted to see how I'd react to you showing up on my doorstep. And you wanted to see if I had a boyfriend." She crossed her arms in front of her tightly stretched T-shirt, which read "New York City." She wore shredded denim shorts and a pair of Keds with no socks. Her makeup was light and fresh, complete with her notorious bright red lipstick. Merek thought she was gorgeous.

Merek shrugged. "You can throw me out anytime

and tell me to leave."

"Don't be silly. You're stuck with me." She laughed. "You just hopped on a plane and came here? Just like that?" She snapped her fingers.

Merek nodded. "Yes. I wanted to see you. I am staying at a hotel nearby."

She walked to him and put her arms around his neck. "I'll have to stop by for a visit." They kissed deeply.

"Moooohhaaaam!" Sally shrieked from behind.

Natalie turned to the girl. "Now, Sally. It's okay. Remember, I told you all about him. I met him in Kentucky when I was cleaning out Grandma and Grandpa's store a long time ago. And Merek came and watched me sing in Columbus. We're good friends. In fact, Merek is my boyfriend."

Sally glared at him Her face was red. "But he's ugly, and he doesn't look like Daddy."

"Sally. That is so rude, young lady. He is handsome, and you're right that he looks, absolutely, nothing like your father. Now, you go to your room and I'll come in and we'll have a talk about this. Okay?"

The cell on the countertop buzzed. Natalie glanced at the number and frowned. "Did you call your father?" she asked the pouting girl.

Sally nodded. "Dad needs to know this man's in our house," she said.

"I see. Let's go to your room right now, young lady. Excuse me, Merek. Make yourself at home."

"Maybe I should leave," Merek said.

"No, I'll be back in a while. Please, make yourself at home," Natalie said.

He wondered if he *should* leave as he looked after Natalie and Sally. He strolled into the living room and stood for a few seconds, staring at the door. He turned and sat in a chair. He picked up a magazine and glanced through it. The home was nice, but not as glamorous as he'd envisioned. He thought his condo in Clintonville was nicer. But this was Manhattan.

The room was neat and clean, with a touch of kids sprinkled in. The carpet was duller in high-traffic areas, a baseball glove was on the couch, and a coloring book and crayons were on the floor. He suspected Natalie had a cleaning woman. She never mentioned a nanny, but it wouldn't surprise him. He thought again what it would be like to have two young children to raise—another man's children. These children. Right now, he talked funny, he was ugly, cool, confused, and the father knew he was there.

"*Dobry Boże*. Maybe Emma was right," he said aloud.

Tuesday

MARY AND SAMUEL sat on Mary's sun porch overlooking the golf course. They ate omelets and pastries that John had made to order. Mary flipped through the latest issue of *Golf Lovers Digest* while she sipped a Bloody Mary.

Samuel glanced out the window. Birds hopped, flew, and sang, and the greens sparkled in the Tuesday morning sun after yesterday's storm. "This is such an incredibly beautiful place you have, Mary," he said.

She closed the magazine and set it aside. "Thank you. I knew exactly what I wanted, and I got it. I planned this course for years. And the additions to the house. At least this and Charles and you came out of my wretched marriage to that worthless farmer. For some unfortunate reason, he's been on my mind lately." She took a gulp of her drink.

"They say every cloud has a silver lining," he said.

She tapped a red fingernail against her glass. John entered the room carrying a silver pot of coffee.

"I'm glad Mary got back in touch. It's wonderful to have you here again," John said to Samuel.

"Thank you, John. A pleasure seeing you again, too.

I'm having a fine visit. I'll be heading back to England on Sunday morning."

Mary sat straight in her chair and glared at Samuel.

"I see. Always nice to go home after a vacation. If you need anything before you leave, please let me know. Would you like more coffee?" John said.

"Yes, thank you. Your cooking hasn't changed. It was all as delicious as I recall," Samuel said.

John nodded. "Thank you, sir." He poured Samuel's coffee then turned to Mary. "Would you like another drink?"

"I don't believe so. Samuel and I will be playing a round before it gets too hot," Mary said.

"I'm not in the mood for golf today. I was hoping we could go see some more of the sights. I'd like to go to the conservatory in Columbus. I read they're having an orchid exhibit," Samuel said.

"You didn't tell me you were leaving Sunday. That's preposterous," Mary blurted.

He turned and looked at her. "I did tell you. You simply must've forgotten." He gave her a quick smile.

She looked away. "I did not forget, because you never told me." She finished her drink and slammed the glass on the table. "Samuel, I need to practice. I have another tournament soon, so we will play golf. You can see all you need to see of America when you come with me on my next tour. It's in California in three weeks. I'm sure they have orchids there," Mary said.

John made a quick exit.

Tense energy filled the room before Samuel said in a measured tone, "Mary, I have truly enjoyed our visit, but I need to get home. And I really don't have the funds to return soon. I'm sorry."

"Funds?" She laughed. "Funds? My dear Samuel, you don't need any *bloody* funds. My God, man. Don't you see? I'm going to pay for everything. Anything you want. All I want you to do is stay here."

Samuel looked at her. "I'm not comfortable with that arrangement."

"What do you mean? I'm offering to take care of you, Samuel. Don't you see? I'm offering to marry you."

"Marry me? You're proposing to me?" Samuel asked.

"Yes. I've been thinking it over and it would be the best thing for both of us. I won't play golf forever and we're both alone. I have all the money we'd ever need."

"I'm flattered at the offer, Mary, but it's not as easy as that."

"Why not?" she asked. "What do you have back in England that's so important?"

"I have my life and my students. I still tutor. You know that."

"Rubbish. You can tutor here. And you won't have to tutor. You won't need any money," she said.

"Mary, I'm not sure how to put this, but I'm not in love with you. I enjoy your company, but—"

"Love? Oh, Samuel. Don't be so naïve. This has nothing to do with love. Not at our age. This is about companionship. I'm offering you the opportunity of your lifetime."

"I understand that. But I'm not comfortable with that arrangement, and I'm simply not sure that we would make good companions."

"What? What do you mean? You just told John that you were having a fine time. And we have been. At least I thought we were, even though you've stayed in the guest room the entire time and not knocked on my bedroom door once."

"I have been having a wonderful time. And I'm grateful for the invitation here. But this wasn't my intention. You're a dear friend, Mary, but—"

"I can't believe you!" Mary cut him off. "We used to be more than friends."

"That was a different time, Mary. Things change."

She stood and walked toward the doorway. She turned and said, "They have pills for that, Samuel. I'll let you think about my offer. I'm sure you'll come to your senses. Cancel your plane ticket and we'll make our engagement announcement Saturday evening at the dinner party."

She turned and left Samuel staring blankly out the window.

Thursday

EMMA SAT ON HER love seat in her condo. Millie had her head in Emma's lap, and Emma petted the basset's long, soft ears.

"Uncle Charles is coming, baby girl. It'll be nice to have him home again, won't it?"

Thump. Thump. Thump. Millie's tail whacked the couch.

"Yes, it will be good to have him home. We can go kayaking and camping and he will bring you lots of cookies."

Millie jumped off the couch and ran in circles, barking.

"You want a cookie?"

Baaaaahrooooo! Bark. Bark. Bark. The air from her tail created a breeze.

Emma laughed. "All right, let's go get a cookie."

Millie ran into the kitchen with Emma close behind. Millie stared at the cookie jar on the counter. Emma reached into the jar and gave the dog a treat.

Ping. Emma's phone alerted her of a text. *Be there in 10. Can't wait to see you.*

Millie walked to her bowl and slurped water as

Emma pulled out snacks she'd prepared for Charles's visit. A few minutes later, the doorbell buzzed and Millie followed Emma into the living room.

Emma opened the door, and she and Charles stood on her small front stoop hugging. "I'm so glad to see you. Come inside before the neighbors start talking."

He followed her inside and she closed the door. "It's so wonderful to see you, too. I forgot how green and lush Ohio is this time of year," he said looking around her condo. "I see you're still saving money on decorating. It's just as lovely as I remember." He grinned.

"Oh, you!" she said.

Millie barked, jumped on Charles, and wagged her tail. He squatted to greet her. "And how have you been, Mildred? I'll bet you've been a good girl." She put her front paws on his knees. Her paws covered his kneecaps. She wiggled, wagged her tail, and licked his face as if it were an ice cream cone. Charles scratched and petted her.

"Yes, sweetheart. I've missed you, too." He stood and followed Emma into the kitchen. "Just let me freshen up after all these kisses," he said. He went into the small bathroom off the hallway.

When he walked into the kitchen, Emma said, "She got pretty excited when I explained that you're moving back here."

"It is good to be home. I'd also forgotten about how these soaring July temperatures feel." He lifted the collar of his starched, white dress shirt several times. "That's one reason why we loved kayaking on the New this time of year. You get cooled off in those rapids. Speaking of which, have the authorities apprehended Earl Calhoon?"

Emma shook her head as she arranged the food and two champagne flutes on the island. "No, and I don't want to talk about it right now. Did you buy the house?"

"Not yet, but I intend to put an offer on it. It's as perfect as the realtor described. It's tastefully decorated, beautifully landscaped, a fenced yard for the boys, and it's a ranch-style with plenty of space for Father and I to have our privacy. The laundry room is on the main living area. It even has a den and a library. A charming brick that backs into the daffodil garden along the park of roses."

"Those are nice," she said. She was going to tell him again how sorry she was about Sam but decided against it. She had sent several cards and flowers after he called with the sad news. "I bought champagne to celebrate, but you'll have to open the bottle. It always scares me."

Charles laughed. "How thoughtful of you, Emma. I can understand why you've shied away from the task since you shattered my dining room mirror, which I had shipped from Italy, I might add. I'll be happy to do the honors."

"Thanks for *that* reminder," she said. She reached into the refrigerator and pulled out the bottle. Charles popped the cork and filled the glasses. He handed one to Emma.

"To your coming home to Clintonville," she said. They clinked glasses and sipped their drinks.

"Okay, I have to get this out here, right now," she said, setting her glass on the counter. "I'm surprised you're moving back here. I mean, I'm really glad, but there's so many memories of Simon here. Even if you left Switzerland, I really didn't expect you to move back here."

"Mother said the same thing. And I agree, but I attended counseling while I've been in Switzerland. It helped me tremendously. I'm finally over him and what happened. My relationship with Father has helped me to realize that love comes in many forms, not just in romantic relationships. Now, it's my turn. Why aren't you in Europe with Stratton?" Charles picked up a cracker.

Emma shrugged. "I wanted to be home with Millie. Europe is Europe. It's nice to visit, but Stratton's practically living there. I don't want to live there. I belong here. Just like you. It's home."

"Indeed." He gazed around the kitchen. "Do you miss him?"

"Yes, but he'll be back soon. I have Merek and Millie and now you to keep me company until he gets here." She never told Charles that she had asked Stratton to move back to West Virginia before he left for Europe, to have some space between them.

"True." He paused and spread cheese onto the cracker. "Have you seen Ron?" Charles asked, focusing on his cracker and trying to sound nonchalant.

Emma tilted her head and looked at him. "No. Why do you ask? Have you?"

Ron Tran and Charles had an on-again, off-again relationship after Simon left. Ron even left his job at Bridge Systems where he worked for Charles, so that they could continue their relationship. But Simon had called Charles for dinner, and Charles didn't tell Ron about it in the best way. But Simon never showed for dinner because he'd been killed.

"No. He made it crystal clear he never wanted me to contact him again. I can't say that I blame him, but it was disturbing the way our relationship ended, his telling me off at a gas station. How degrading for both of us. I do wish he'd speak with me. It's always concerned me. Ron's a wonderful person, and I, well …" He looked away.

Emma reached across the countertop and covered his hand. She loved this man with every cell in her soul, and she was elated that he was moving back. She had missed him more than words could describe. Two years ago, Charles moved to Switzerland and Merek went back to Poland. Even though she and Stratton were getting along well—and he was living with her at the time—she had been devastated. She thought she'd lost them both. Now, both of them were going to be back in Clintonville.

"I'd be glad to talk to him for you," she said.

"You would? Oh, Emma, I don't expect you to get involved."

"I know. But think about it. We're all here to help each other. I don't mind. I like Ron, too," she said.

"That's kind of you. I'll give it some thought."

Millie came into the kitchen and trotted to her bed to take a nap. Emma and Charles continued to catch up. An hour later, they laughed at Millie's snoring. He checked his Cartier watch.

"Oh, look at the time. It's nearly four. Emma, I have to run. I have a dinner appointment this evening, but I wanted to stop by since I was in the neighborhood. I'm staying at the Leveque, much to Mother's chagrin. I have several meetings downtown so it was simply much easier to stay there. And since Samuel is at Mother's, I certainly don't want to intrude on whatever *this* visit is about. I needed time alone, quite frankly."

Emma woke Mille and the two showed Charles to the door.

"I'll see you Saturday at the party," he said. They hugged. "It is truly wonderful to be in Clintonville again."

***

"Hello, Melissa. How are you?" James Mars leaned into the computer screen.

"I'm fine, but you'll have to back up a little. I can only see your chin." Other voices rose and fell in the background as James sat back in his chair.

"How's this?" he asked.

"Better," Melissa said. She turned away from the screen. "Hey, Josh. Come say hello to Grandpa Mars."

Grandpa Mars. Poor kids need to keep their grandparents straight now. It's just not right, James thought.

Off-screen he heard Josh say, "But, Mom, I don't want to talk to him."

"Come on, now. Grandpa Mars is busy, so he doesn't have a lot of time. Come talk to him. Look into the screen," James heard Melissa say, her head turned away.

After several seconds of commotion, Joshua Mars-Mendoza's face appeared on the screen looking clearly miffed.

"Hi, Grandpa."

"Hello, Josh. How are you?" James asked, excitedly.

The boy frowned sideways and shrugged. "I'm okay." He turned and whined, "But I don't want to …" to Melissa. James could hear Melissa prodding Josh to talk and more argument erupted between them.

Josh turned back to the computer. "How are you, Grandpa Mars?" he finally moaned.

"Just fine. Just fine. Thanks for asking. How have you been? What have you been up to?" James said with a huge smile.

The boy shrugged. "Nothin,' I gotta go now."

Melissa's face filled the screen. "I'm sorry, James. You know how kids are."

She calls me James now, instead of Dad. Ever since she married that man, Carlos. James fumed inside.

"I certainly do. How are things in Arizona? Is Kassandra available?"

"Things are good. It's hot here, but it's summer in Arizona. Can't expect anything else." She paused, not knowing what else to say. "She's not here. She's at a friend's. Is there something you needed?"

"No. No, not at all. I just miss you and my grandchildren and wanted to say hello. I'm still getting the hang of this skyping thing. George—down at the marina—his grandson is still giving me tips. It's nice we can do this. See each other while we talk. Lucy sends her love."

Melissa looked blank. "How is she?"

"She's fine. They take very good care of her. Say, you and the kids want to come and stay for a couple weeks? We could all go visit her. It'd be good for Lucy. It would be wonderful. She'd be so happy. I could take us all out on the boat and we could fish. We could ski—"

"Sorry, James, we can't," Lucy interrupted. "The kids will be starting school again in a few weeks. They have baseball and soccer games. And Carlos is busy with the construction business. You wouldn't believe how it's booming out here. We can't just up and leave."

"Oh. I understand. I see. Yes. Booming. I've read about it."

"It's just hard to get away. You understand." She dropped her voice and moved a little closer to the screen. "Our lives are here now. I'll never let them forget Jimmy, but life goes on. You need to move on, too." She looked sad.

James said nothing. What she was really saying was, he needed to leave them alone.

"Maybe you can fly out for Christmas. It's cold in Ohio. There's a hotel not ten minutes away," she said.

"We'll see," he replied. "Yes, maybe Lucy and I could come visit." *And stay at a hotel and not at your house,* he thought, raging inside.

"That'd be nice. Hey, I have to run. It's been great talking with you. Take care, James."

"You too, Melissa. Lucy and I send our love."

"You, too. Bye."

The computer screen went blank.

James Mars shut down his computer and crossed his arms in front of his chest. "Skyping is no way to see *my* grandchildren."

Saturday, August 2

THE ROAR OF the crowd grew louder throughout the evening. There were over a hundred people at Mary's party. A few celebrities she golfed with were huddled together by the rock fireplace. Charles had collected most of the stones on kayak trips with Emma over the years.

"I put an offer on the house this morning," Charles said to Emma.

She hugged him. "That's awesome. It's official. You're moving back home."

"Yes, I am. I do love Switzerland and thought I would stay there. It's beautiful in a crisp, clean, intense way. And the country is quite progressive. But Clintonville is home."

Emma nodded as she glanced across the room at Joey, who sat in a chair with his leg propped on a stool. Dr. Amy Fields sat next to him in another chair.

"I've never seen this staff working here before. Did Mary fire John?" Emma asked Charles.

He shook his head. "No, John and his wife are over there. They're guests this evening, thanks to my suggestion. Mary hired a caterer."

"That's pretty amazing," Emma said.

"I agree. It's a shame that Stratton and Merek couldn't attend. I look forward to seeing them," Charles said.

"Merek's only texted me once since he left on Tuesday. He said they had been doing a lot of sightseeing in the city—*with the kids*. I hope he doesn't move to New York."

"You don't own him, Emma," Charles said.

"That's what Joey keeps telling me. I know, I know. It's just ..."

"I was surprised he didn't stay in Poland, quite honestly," Charles said. He took a sip of beer.

"Me, too. But I was sure happy when he came back," Emma said. She sipped her Côtes-du-Rhône. "I'm selfish. I know."

"Yes, Emma, sometimes you are. We all are. Not to change this delightful confessional conversation of yours, but I'd like to introduce you to my former tutor. Samuel. Without him, I doubt I would be an engineer."

They walked over to Samuel, who sat beside Mary on one of the sofas. As they talked, a couple entered the room. Emma glanced up to see Merek and Natalie. She went to greet them.

"You're here! Natalie. It's great to see you two," Emma said, hugging her.

"*Tak*. I told Natalie about the party, and we wanted to come. So, we are here," Merek said, putting his arms around the two women's waists.

"It's good to see you, too," Natalie said to Emma. "Mike has the kids this weekend, so we decided, why not? This place is extraordinary. I can't wait to meet Mary and Charles. I know nothing about golf, but Mike was impressed when I told him where we were going. He knows all about Mary Wellington."

"Did Mike meet Merek?" Emma asked.

"Yes. He went with me when we dropped off Kenny and Sally."

"And everything's ... *okay*?" Emma asked.

Natalie gave Emma an understanding look. "Yes and no. Mike's remarried with his own life, so he can't tell me how to live mine. And Kenny adores Merek. Sally, on the other hand... She'll come around. Merek will win her over."

"It's got to be sort of hard for kids of divorced parents. I don't mean to sound harsh or anything, but you know what I mean," Emma said.

"I certainly do. When Mike remarried, the kids weren't keen at all on getting a new mom. But they're fine with it now. And Merek isn't your ordinary guy."

"You can say that again," Emma agreed. They laughed.

"Mr. Joey, he is here, too," Merek said, waving to Joey.

"Yep. With *his doctor*. The young cute gal sitting beside him. She's the one he wouldn't tell Merek and me about in the hospital."

Merek smiled. "Ahhhh. Yes." He gave Joey a nod and a thumbs-up from across the room. Joey did the same to Merek.

"I'm flying solo tonight. Stratton's still in Europe, but he'll be home soon."

Natalie put her hand on Emma's arm. "That's good. I'm sure you miss him."

"Yeah, I do. Let me introduce you to some folks," she said to Natalie. "Merek, I'm stealing your woman."

"That is fine, Miss H. I want to thank Miss Mary for

inviting us and talk to Mr. Joey and Mr. Charles."

"I'm sure she'll be thrilled you made the trip from New York. It'll probably be in the tabloids," Emma said. She grabbed Natalie's hand, and they made their way through the crowd while the band started another song.

"Merek Polanski. You did make it. And is that pretty lady with Emma your friend from New York?" Mary asked.

"Yes. She is New York Natalie. She has stolen my heart." Merek put his hands over his heart and leaned back.

"I can understand. Merek, you remember Samuel. You met him at Weiland's."

"Yes. Mr. Samuel. So nice to see you again." They shook hands and the three of them chatted. A few people danced in front of the fireplace. Merek left them and made his way to Joey and Amy. He shook Joey's hand and Joey introduced Merek to Amy.

"So nice to meet such a beautiful lady," Merek said, kissing the top of Amy's hand.

"What a gentleman." She lightly punched Joey on the shoulder. "Pay attention Lieutenant Reed. You could learn something here."

"Look out. I think Merek's trying to pull some Polish stuff on you. Don't get any ideas, Mr. Polanski," Joey said, jokingly. Merek sat beside him in another chair.

"Did you find out who ran over you?" Merek asked. Joey shook his head. "No, not yet."

Merek nodded in deep thought. "I am sorry."

"Yeah. This may be an open case for a long time," Joey said.

Merek sipped a beer and scanned the crowd. Natalie and Emma were across the room, talking with Charles and Mary.

Joey interrupted his thoughts. "Natalie is beautiful and a great singer," he said.

"*Tak*. She is the one, Mr. Joey. I feel it."

"Sort of complicated, isn't it? She lives in Manhattan and has a couple kids? An ex-husband around. How you going to swing all that?" Joey asked.

Merek shrugged and said, "Love will make it work."

Joey nodded. "I'm sure it will, my friend. I'm sure it will."

They stopped talking and continued to people-watch. The increasing volume of party noise made it difficult to have a conversation.

Emma and Natalie made their way back to Joey and Merek. Introductions were made.

"Hey, I need a little break from all this. I think I'll go out on the sun porch," Joey said.

"Sure thing, Mr. Joey," Merek said.

"May I join you?" Charles appeared.

"I wouldn't have it any other way," Joey said. They made their way to the sun porch and settled into the furniture. Charles closed the sliding glass doors.

"Ahhh. This is much better. It's getting too loud in there," Emma said.

"I couldn't hear a thing," Amy agreed.

Charles and Merek hugged and talked as a flock of Canada geese flew over the golf course in front of a beautiful sunset. "I've not seen that in a long time," Natalie said, watching the birds pass. "I miss nature. I need to get Sally and Kenny to the park more."

"I love birds," Emma said.

"I don't know the first thing about them," Amy added. "I can't say I'm a fan. I think they're noisy and messy."

"They are." Emma agreed. "I've never seen a better example of that than at James Mars's house."

"Who's James Mars?" Natalie asked.

"He's a retired cop that has a boat on the lake where Joey got run over. I kayaked to his house again on Monday."

"You didn't mention that. I thought I told you the guys at the station would handle it," Joey said.

Emma shrugged. "It doesn't matter. I never got to talk to him. There was no one at home. But the birds were there. Talk about a mess. They even pooped on *Arlene*. I had to wash her off when I got home." Emma explained to Amy and Natalie that *Arlene* was her kayak's name.

"When I was at the marina, I saw a car covered in bird *gówno*," Merek added.

"See, like I said. Birds are just messy," Amy said.

"Yes, I loathe parking my car under trees in the summer. Anyway, I'm pleased that Mother had such a nice turnout this evening," Charles said, changing the subject. He took a drink of beer.

"So what's it like being the son of the world's best senior golfer?" Natalie asked Charles.

He smiled. "It was quite interesting, to say the least. If she wasn't traveling, she was here playing golf with people from all over the world. Mary is just … Mary," Charles replied.

"Was that Robert Plant I saw leaning against the fireplace?" Amy asked.

"Yes. They play golf together, occasionally. One of the Rolling Stones will be arriving later. She golfs with them all. I can't remember which one is going to be here this evening. I believe it's Ron Wood."

"Oh, my God. Wait. Stop. You're kidding! This is totally unbelievable," Natalie said. "Maybe your mother would introduce me to these people and they could help me get a record contract. I mean, I live in Manhattan, but I've never met *these* kinds of people or even see them. This is incredible."

"You are a beautiful singer," Merek said.

"Yes, you are," Emma agreed. "And a great guitar player. And that's not such a crazy idea. Charles, you should talk to Mary about it."

"I'd be happy to. Mother knows many people. I'm sure she'd be happy to help you in any way possible," Charles said.

"Maybe I could sing this evening, if the band wouldn't mind. Maybe after Ron arrives. Maybe I'll ask them to accompany me. This is so exciting!" Natalie said. "It's unbelievable. I live in New York City and I come to the little town of Circleville, Ohio, and this happens. Merek, you never told me about Mary."

Merek shrugged. "I did not think of these things," he said.

"I think that's an awesome idea," Amy said.

They all agreed and chattered on.

Emma stood and walked over to a window. Charles followed. "A penny for your thoughts, Emma Haines," he said.

"I can feel something in the back of my mind, but …" She stared out the window. Charles sipped his drink and followed her gaze. After several moments, she turned and walked quickly to Joey.

"Joey, that's it!" she said.

"What? What's *it*?" he said.

"I know who ran over you," she said.

All eyes were on her. "James Mars. Those spots on the top of that Bimini. It's bird poop. Just like the bird poop all over his dock. And that car at the marina that Merek saw. It had to be his car. And he was at the station before the accident, talking with Cook and Sammy. Cook mentioned that Mars was there. Maybe one of them told Mars about us kayaking and forgot. It's him, Joey."

"That's crazy, Emma. I don't even know him. There's no motive. And he's a cop."

"Think about it. Didn't you tell me that you and his son were up for the detective promotion and you got it, not him?"

"But that was a long time ago."

"So what! Think about it. You got to work inside at a desk more often as a detective and his son was still on the streets. And he was—"

"Killed … in the line of duty," Joey finished.

"And he was Mars's only kid," Emma said. "How would you feel?"

The room fell silent.

"Let's go talk to him," Emma said. "Right now."

***

James Mars was giddy as he packed his suitcase. He knew in his heart that going to see his grandchildren was the right thing to do. Melissa had planted the seed to go before school started. He needed a vacation and it would be a nice surprise for them.

He checked the clock on the nightstand. He'd watch TV for a while and then go to bed and get a good night's rest. He wouldn't be at church in the morning with Lucy, he'd be at the airport, boarding his plane to Arizona. He decided not to mention it to Lucy, but he did inform the staff at the Alzheimer's center that he was going to Arizona to visit his family and wouldn't be in for at least a week. If Lucy did happen to ask about him—which he doubted—they were not to mention the trip to her because it would just confuse her. The staff agreed.

He walked back into the kitchen with a lilt in his step he hadn't had in years. "I should take them gifts," he said aloud to himself. "I'll just buy something there. Less for the TSA to have to go through. When *was* the last time I flew on a plane?"

He knew the answer to that question. The last time he took Lucy to see the children several years ago. He felt a lurch in his heart knowing that was the last time Lucy would likely see their grandchildren. "But it doesn't mean I can't," he said.

He started to whistle as he scurried around with new found energy. He checked the laundry room for a pair of pants he couldn't find. They were hanging near the dryer. "There you are," he said.

He took the pants from the hanger and headed back toward the bedroom. He stopped in the living room and looked out the bay window at the backyard. Birds sat in the trees and bushes and flew around the empty feeders. A few looked in his direction.

"Tough luck. No one's going to feed you while I'm gone, so get over it. Go eat bugs or something, you spoiled scoundrels" he said. "In fact, when I come home, I'm taking down all those feeders. I don't have time to deal with you anymore."

He walked closer to the window and looked out at the empty dock. His boat was in storage at the marina and he knew that George wouldn't charge him a cent for it when he returned. "George is such a thoughtful man," he said aloud. He started back to the bedroom when the doorbell rang. "Now who could that be? I'll bet it's Sammy or Cook, come to see me off." He smiled.

He opened the door. The smile turned to shock. He recognized the woman and the tattooed man and the man in the arm and leg casts—Joey Reed. His heart sank. He pasted a smile on his face and stood tall. "Yes? May I help you?"

Joey hobbled toward him in his boot and showed his badge. "James Mars?"

"Yes. Of course. I believe we've all met at one time or another," James said with a puzzled look. "What can I do for you, Lieutenant Reed?"

"I'd like to ask you a few questions. May we come in, please?"

"Yes. Of course. I remember you. You were friends with Jimmy. And your friends here were asking about your accident. How may I help you?"

"It's about your boat, sir," Joey said.

James opened the door wide and motioned them into the house. Joey, Emma, and Merek stood in the living room facing him.

"Has it been stolen? I don't understand. It's in storage at the marina," James said.

"No, sir. Your boat has not been reported stolen. I just need to ask you a few questions," Joey said.

"I'd be glad to talk to you, but this is a very bad time. You see, I'm packing to fly to Arizona to visit my grandchildren in the morning. Can this wait until I return?"

"No, sir, I don't believe it can," Joey said. The room fell silent.

James looked at everyone's somber faces for a few

seconds before he burst into tears. He dropped the pants on the floor, held his head in his hands, and bawled uncontrollably. The visitors stood in silence. Merek looked at the floor and walked a few feet away.

Finally, James raised his head and looked at Joey. Tears streamed down his face. "You should've never gotten that promotion. Jimmy was the better man for the job. Not you! Not you! If it wasn't for you, my Jimmy would still be alive and I'd still have my family. Jimmy was killed and caused Lucy to have a breakdown," James sputtered angrily through his tears.

They listened to him sputter and weep.

Finally, Joey asked, "How did you know it was me in the kayak?"

James wiped his face and got himself under control.

"I was meeting Sammy and Cook to go to lunch. They were in your office and you were all laughing it up, talking about your going kayaking. You told them exactly when and where you'd be. I stood outside and overheard everything," James said.

"I wasn't going to go out on the lake at all that day, but I did. I watched you and her through Lucy's birding binoculars, out there paddling around the lake without a care in the world, smiling and laughing. The longer I watched you, the madder I got. I became so angry that I revved the engine ..." He dropped his head and began sobbing harder.

"And ran over him," Emma finished.

James nodded. After a long moment, he looked up. "I never planned it, but I just got so mad." He calmed down a bit before he looked at Joey and said, "I'll just get a few things before you take me downtown." He started toward the hallway.

"That won't be necessary, Detective Mars," Joey said. "I'm not pressing charges."

Emma and Merek looked at Joey as if he were an alien.

"I'm not pressing charges," he repeated. "I'm deeply sorry about Jimmy. He was a great cop and I'm sorry. I want you to go to Arizona and enjoy your grandchildren."

James stared at Joey. He walked over and hugged him. Joey held the retired officer as he sobbed.

"Thank you. Thank you," James said through his tears.

Sunday

"I'M SORRY WE left your party so quickly," Emma said to Mary as they ate breakfast. John walked in and placed a small crystal pitcher of maple syrup on the table and refilled everyone's coffee.

"Thank you, John," Mary said.

"And Joey isn't pressing charges?" Charles asked, picking up his coffee cup.

Emma shook her head. "Nope. And I've got to say, I'm proud of him."

"It isn't totally up to him, is it? I mean, don't the courts have something to say about all this? After all, the man attempted to murder a police officer," Mary said.

"I don't know about the specifics, but Joey said he's not pressing charges and is putting it all behind him. He wants to focus on his rehabilitation and getting on with work. With the help of his doctor, of course," Emma said with a grin.

"He was starry-eyed last night," Mary said.

"He wasn't the only one," Charles added, glancing at Mary. "Is Samuel still sleeping?"

Mary placed her fork on her plate and drew a deep

breath. "If he is, he's doing it on a plane to England. He left earlier this morning."

"He's gone?" Charles asked.

"Yes. He had to get back to his students. He's very loyal to his job, you know."

"He is a most excellent tutor. Just look how successful I became," Charles said.

"Oh, brother," Emma said, rolling her eyes.

"Yes, he is. Anyway, we had a nice visit and it was time for him to leave," Mary said, straightening in her chair. She took a long drink of her Bloody Mary.

Charles and Emma shared a look.

"Merek was sorry for leaving last night without saying goodbye. Charles, he told me to thank you for dropping Natalie off at his place," Emma said.

"It was my pleasure. She's quite charming and extremely taken with Merek," Charles said.

Mary said, "Natalie is something else. We had a pleasant talk last night after the three of you ran out of here. She even sang a few songs with the band. She is a talented and beautiful woman. She met the musicians and they talked for some time. Such a life, being from the backwoods of Kentucky. Now, she reeks of Manhattan class. She is taken with Merek, although I can't understand why. They have absolutely nothing in common and they look like a pair of mismatched socks. I would think she'd want a man more like her. Pass the eggs, please, dear." Charles handed Mary the eggs.

"All I know is, I hope they commute for a looooong time," Emma said. "If they don't, he'll have to move to New York because she has two kids in school and their father lives there. You're right, though. They really have nothing in common, but they both seem nuts about each other. It'll pass."

"Emma doesn't want to lose him," Charles said, smiling.

"I don't own him," Emma said, spearing a piece of bacon.

"That's true," Charles agreed. "Emma, I must say, I'm still intrigued about how you identified who ran over Lieutenant Reed by the bird droppings on the Bimini. Bravo, my dear." He put his fork on his plate and clapped his hands. "Bravo."

She smiled. "Thanks. It all just clicked when we were sitting around talking last night. Especially when Merek mentioned seeing Mars's car covered in bird poop at the marina. If the birds pooped all over his car and his dock, they'd poop on his boat, especially if he didn't park it under the boat port. They're not that picky about where they do their business. It would be a part-time job keeping everything clean. Mars washed and waxed the boat several times after he hit Joey, but he didn't think about the Bimini or his car," Emma said.

"Revolting," Charles shuddered. "A dirty vehicle says a great deal about a person," he added.

"All my vehicles, including my golf carts, are washed at least five times a week by my staff," Mary said.

After they finished breakfast, Emma turned to Charles and asked, "Want to go kayaking today?"

TO BE CONTINUED

About the Author

Trudy Brandenburg is an avid kayaker, writer, and birder. Over the past twenty years, she has paddled on many rivers and lakes, the North Atlantic and North Pacific oceans, and the Gulf of Mexico. She is a member of the Southern Ohio Floaters Association (SOFA) kayaking club, based in her hometown of Chillicothe, Ohio.

She's been a researcher and writer at an insurance company for nearly thirty years and is a member of Buckeye Crime Writers. Her published works have appeared in various publications. This is her fourth novel in *The Emma Haines Kayak Mystery Series*.

When she's not writing, kayaking, bird watching, bicycle riding, reading, or creating her designer greeting cards, you may see her strolling through Clintonville, Ohio, or shopping at Weiland's Market.

For current information and to request book signings, speaking engagements or writing class instruction, email her through the contact link on her website.

http://trudybrandenburg.wix.com/trudybrandenburg

The Emma Haines Kayak Mystery Series

In Order

Nighthawks on the New River

Peacocks on Paint Creek

Robins on the Red River

Osprey on O'Shaughnessy Reservoir

Made in the USA
Monee, IL
14 July 2023